COLD ATTRACTION

A SCIFI ALIEN ROMANCE

ZOE ASHWOOD

Edited by Emmy Ellis (StudioENP)

Proofread by Lori Parks (LesCourt Author Services)

Cover by Elle Thorpe (Images for Authors)

Created with Vellum

*For my husband, who
discussed alien planets with me.*

1

Adriana

"*ALL CREW REPORT TO POSITIONS. Countdown to landing: seventeen minutes.*"

The loud tinny voice echoed through the speakers, startling Adriana into a twitch. Since she was in the process of applying cherry-red lipstick, this meant she now had a smudge of color drawn outside her lip line. Cursing under her breath, she wiped it all off and reapplied. Then she studied her reflection in the mirror and decided it would have to do for now.

No way was she missing landing on an alien planet because she was obsessing over lipstick.

Now, some people might say that putting on makeup before disembarking on a world where no human had ever walked before was an unnecessary affectation. But those people didn't see the sneer that Captain Taron ad Naals gave her the last time she saw him in the ship's corridor. She would look fabulous and put-together for their next meeting.

Not that it was easy to look fabulous when wearing two layers of thermal clothes, snow pants, snow boots, and a thick down parka. Adriana was concerned about fitting through doorways with this much gear on. But since they were entering Rendian atmosphere at the time of their late autumn, this was the only way for humans to survive. Daytime temperatures were way below freezing, they'd been told, and nights got even colder.

It would be an experience to write home about. Literally. She intended to compose an article about the alien society and publish it the moment she returned to Earth in three months. It would be the making of her academic career. She might even get a book deal out of it.

That should be enough to impress Mom and Dad. The thought was insidious and unwelcome—and the therapist she'd been required to see during her preparation for this mission had urged her to stop making decisions based on her parents' wishes. She was an independent woman, one of the best scholars in her field. This was the chance of a lifetime, and she would make the most of it.

She swiped her electronic cuff over the control panel, and the door of her cramped cabin slid noiselessly to the side, revealing the controlled chaos beyond. Humans and Rendians alike were moving toward the bridge, and she joined the stream, waddling along, already sweating under all the layers.

The large chamber at the front of the spaceship was crammed with working crew members and observers, the latter pressed up against the spherical glass to enjoy the view.

And oh, what a view it was.

Rendu, a planet slightly smaller than Earth, was approaching rapidly, growing larger by the second. Its atmosphere was shrouded in clouds, with only flashes of white peeking through.

Adriana's breath caught, and she drifted toward the glass in a sort of trance, until she placed her palm flat on the cold surface separating her from deep space. Up until this moment, the trip from Earth had seemed like a dream, a fantastical journey through the stars, especially since they'd traveled at superluminal speed. But now their destination was near, she felt the weight of responsibility. They were entering a new *world*. How would they ever be able to document it all in three months before their return to Earth?

"Adriana!" At a low hiss from her right, she tore her gaze away from the planet and glanced over to find her two colleagues waving her to join them.

Like her, Mika and Hanne were part of the ten-person unit that had been given permission to visit Rendu for an exploratory mission. A zoologist and an astrophysicist, they'd become her friends during the months of grueling physical preparations, during nights spent studying everything they knew about the faraway planet.

Now they were staring at her like she'd lost her mind.

"What the hell are you wearing?" Mika asked, blunt as ever, her Japanese translating seamlessly through the incredibly handy translation devices the aliens had handed out like candy as soon as they'd arrived on Earth.

It was then that Adriana noticed she was the only one wrapped in winter gear while the rest of the passengers and crew were in light uniforms and casual clothes.

"But I thought—" She narrowed her eyes at Ben, the doctor who was responsible for keeping the human crew healthy. "I was told to prepare for extreme conditions."

Ben elbowed the Rendian on his left. They both looked at her and sniggered.

She gave Ben the finger and turned back to her friends. "I'm going to kill him."

Of course, Captain Naals chose that moment to stride onto the Bridge. He never simply *walked*—he was too intense for that. His height alone was enough to dwarf most human men Adriana had seen, and his broad shoulders bore distinctive spikes. Mika and Ben had discussed the Rendian physiology at length, theorizing whether those spikes—and the ones running down the aliens' spines—were bone or horn, but hadn't come close enough to any of the crew members to really check. And the crew always wore the light slate-gray uniforms, so it wasn't as though they put their bodies on display for the humans to study.

Adriana had touched Captain Naals' spikes once and could confirm they were probably bone, even though she only felt them through his uniform, but that would mean admitting to having been in close proximity with the captain, so she'd kept it to herself. She didn't know what her teammates would think of her if she revealed what had happened.

Taron ad Naals crossed the distance from the door to his captain's chair, folding himself into the throne-like seat with grace that was at odds with his impressively built body. His every movement spoke of restraint and authority, and his form was one honed by years of training. Accepting a command tablet from an officer, he scanned whatever data needed his approval and murmured something in reply.

Adriana imagined the low rasp of his voice and shivered despite being hopelessly overheated in all those clothes.

Captain Naals' frosty gaze zeroed in on her, and his light-blue eyes narrowed. Adriana had the sudden urge to run over and sit on his lap so she could run her fingers through his long white hair, and barely stopped herself. She didn't know whether the captain sensed her need, but his pale lips pressed into a thin line. Then he simply looked away.

Ouch.

Adriana swallowed the lump of hurt that constricted her throat, determined not to let him ruin this once-in-a-lifetime experience for her. She wouldn't think about him, even if the thought of the kiss they'd shared still had her heart racing.

Kiss, singular. She needed to remember that. He'd kissed her once, and she could have sworn he'd been just as passionate about it as her, but he hadn't spoken a word to her since.

The last thing she wanted was to alert her crew members that she was moping because of his rejection. She squared her shoulders, turned her back on him, and wedged herself between her friends.

Taking both their hands, she released a shuddering sigh and was grateful when they both squeezed her fingers.

"This is it, ladies. We're not on Earth anymore."

2

Taron

HIS HUMAN WAS IGNORING HIM. She'd put on her winter clothing, and he had to suppress the twitch that threatened to curl his lips when he caught sight of her. Would she roll around like a ball if he tipped her to the side? At least he wouldn't have to worry about her getting lost in the snow—with her lime-green coat, she'd be visible for miles in the barren landscape.

He wished he could get to know her better. He wished he could peel off those clothes and revel in the gorgeous body hiding beneath them.

He'd start by kissing her again, then lick all the parts of her that made her moan. He'd never seen such dark hair, and he knew instinctively she'd respond to him immediately if he speared his fingers into that thick, shiny mass. Her brown eyes would go round and wide, and her lips would part... She'd open up to him like she had the day before everything turned to shit.

He'd had to stay away from her, even though he'd developed a strange feeling inside his chest that worsened the farther away he was from her. Granted, he couldn't go very far on his ship—he was aware of her whereabouts *all the time*—but he needed to put some distance between them the moment they landed in the capital.

He couldn't afford distractions, not when his nation might be on the verge of a civil war.

Pulling himself out of the daydream with a sigh, he signaled to his lieutenant to prepare the ship for landing. The news they'd received halfway through their trip back to Rendu had rattled the crew members; their faces were drawn with worry, and they were all eager to return home and check their loved ones were safe.

The spaceship pierced the cloud cover, the entrance into the planet's atmosphere seamless and smooth. From the humans' astonished expressions, he understood that they'd expected something much more violent. But after hundreds of similar trips, he and his crew knew how to handle this old beauty. And he might have spoken to his crew earlier, asking them to make an extra effort for the human crew. No need to scare them further—their faces were slack-jawed with awe and astonishment as they stared out toward the city of Volarun.

Pride rushed through him at the sight, and he tried putting himself in their shoes. How could they not admire the tall obsidian spires of the fortress rising from the snow-covered plains? Or the massive horseshoe ridge of the Dozois mountains that sheltered the capital from the worst of the ice storms?

But his heart was heavy when they approached. Worry

had kept him up for most of the nights since receiving the short missive, its pared-down contents relaying a chilling scenario: *King dead. Regent Gilmar has Queen Z.*

The message had been sent through the Volarun's main communication satellite, the massive bird orbiting Rendu being the only piece of machinery able to penetrate the depths of deep space and contact ships light-years away, even if the memos needed to be short.

It was the last word they'd received from Rendu, and Taron expected the worst. If his brothers couldn't even respond to his increasingly urgent messages, the situation in the capital had to be dire. The missive he'd received suggested that Gilmar had had a hand in ensuring the king's death. If that was so, he would murder the bastard the moment he arrived at the palace. Outrage threatened to overwhelm him, so he drew a deep breath to keep his anger from showing on his face.

He hadn't made an announcement to the humans yet, so everyone, including Adriana, was flying in blind. And Taron wasn't certain he could ensure the humans' safety if the monarch who'd authorized their entry to the planet was deceased. The thought twisted his insides, and he glanced at Adriana again. If they were boarded at landing, he'd have to move quickly to get to her before—

"The tower is not responding, sir," his junior lieutenant informed him in an undertone. "What are your orders?"

Taron scanned the sky port's many platforms, some empty and others carrying spacecraft of various shapes and sizes. "There." Pointing to an empty platform as far away as possible from the tower command center, he muttered, "Have the crew prepare for a hostile situation. Armor up, spears charged for stunning only." If they were going into battle, he would not be sending his crew in unprepared.

The junior lieutenant's eyes widened. "Yes, sir."

With one last glance at Adriana, he tapped a command into his electronic cuff, and the soft fabric of his captain's uniform took on a metallic sheen. The integrated armor molded itself to his body like a second skin, the collar creeping up his neck to protect all vital parts. He wouldn't put on his helmet until after landing, but barring a direct hit to the head, he was now more or less invulnerable.

The problem was, their potential attackers had access to all the same gear. And they had the numbers on their side. If only he knew what they were getting into...

A gasp startled him from his thoughts. Adriana was looking straight at him, her red lips parted in shock. He cursed inwardly; her gaze slid down his body—but not in a way he enjoyed. She'd noticed something had changed. He shook his head at her, warning her not to speak, but he really should have known better than to expect her obedience.

The woman opened her mouth, and her clear voice cut through the hushed chatter on the Bridge. "What is going on?"

3

Adriana

ALL HEADS TURNED TOWARD HER, and then, when they saw where she was staring, snapped to watch Captain Naals. Instinctively, she moved closer to the rest of their group and felt her crew's presence behind her.

The captain was wearing some sort of armor when minutes ago, his uniform had seemed perfectly ordinary. A closer examination of his officers revealed that they'd all donned similar protection—or at least she assumed that was what the shiny metallic coating was all about.

"Why are you putting on armor?" Hanne asked.

Adriana grabbed her hand and then took Mika's, too, for good measure.

"And why is that guy over there holding a spear?" Mika added.

Their hands squeezed hers, and a tremor shook her body. This didn't look good.

"Nothing to worry about." The woman on the captain's right, a slender Rendian beauty with the lieutenant's marks on her shoulder, spread her arms slightly in what was probably supposed to be a calming gesture. Instead, the blue glint of light on her armor only made her look more inhuman. "Just standard procedure."

"Why don't we get armor, then?" Adriana stepped forward, releasing her friends' hands and immediately regretted it, fidgeting under the captain's cool stare. "Will the landing be dangerous?"

"We will protect you." His voice allowed no argument, but he hadn't exactly answered her question.

"What do we need protection from?" She thought she saw his jaw clench at her insistence. "And why weren't we informed of this?"

"Because you're under my command." Those words, if spoken in a different tone, would have had her squirming in anticipation. But not now. Now, she was worried about her safety. Some deep part of her wanted to believe him when he said he would protect her—*them*, protect *them*, as in all the human crew, not just her, how selfish was she? But rationally, their armor and the strange, restless energy coursing through the room did nothing to calm her fears.

"With all due respect, Captain, we would like to be informed about any such developments in the future."

"You, madam, need to *respect* the chain of command and understand that we would not intentionally put you in danger," he shot back, his white, straight eyebrows furrowing in a scowl. "Now stand down and let us handle this situation so we can all come out of it alive."

Her colleagues muttered around her, their faces anxious as they turned back toward the glass wall. She kept her gaze pinned on the captain, though, watched him as he issued commands to his well-trained crew. The entire team moved like a machine, every member certain of their place on the *Stargazer*, the sleek ship that brought them to this planet.

What should have been a joyous moment, an epic pinpoint in human history, had become fraught with fear. Damn him, damn him for not being open with them. She'd thought they were developing a relationship of some sort—perhaps 'friendship' was a strong word, but she respected him, especially after she saw how his crew obeyed him. She'd hoped to earn his respect, but that didn't seem to be on the program for today.

If she was being completely honest, she'd been in danger of developing a massive crush on the tall alien with his fathomless blue eyes and a reluctant, gorgeous smile. He made her want things she hadn't wanted for years. He stirred something inside her, some inner well of longing that no other man had touched before.

But he'd cut her off completely after their ill-advised kiss, and all her hopes of seeing what was underneath that gray uniform vanished into thin air. She'd only had time to touch his cold skin once, to feel the power in his coiled muscles, to brush her fingertips over his back and shoulders, marveling at how different he was from her, how hard and solid against her softness. Then his communication device had blared to life, interrupting her, and he'd zipped up his shirt, disappearing from her room. And he hadn't returned.

Now, she had a decision to make: did she still trust him enough to stop prodding at this issue? Would knowing what was happening really help their cause?

The honest truth was that out here, with only a handful of humans present, there was no real alternative to this. She hated being forced into a corner, but she wasn't a fool. Once they landed planet-side, their chances of survival without the Rendians' help were slim to none.

Her gaze darted around the spacious Bridge. The technology of the ship, the Rendians' armor, their *weapons* were incomparable to their own. This civilization, small though it was, was advanced beyond all imagination. That a scant million aliens developed gadgets that seven billion humans hadn't managed to build was a humbling thought.

No way would a fight between their races end well for the humans. Especially not when there were only ten of them on this ship.

"Hey, guys," she said, spreading her hands to indicate they should all huddle together. "Let's just trust them for now, yeah? They've treated us well so far. There's nothing we can do, so let's just keep out of their way and be smart."

There was some grumbling, especially from the two SEALs who'd come along for protection—though the Rendians wouldn't allow them to bring any weapons on board. But they all nodded.

Adriana glanced back at Captain Naals and caught a flash of something like approval in his gaze before he looked away again. And damn him, that approval meant everything to her.

The landing was just as calm as their entry into the planet's orbit. The spaceship barely shuddered when it settled in the double claw-like supports. Adriana understood immediately why everyone had laughed at her—they didn't disembark directly onto the landing platform but rather waited for a shiny metal tube to attach itself to the door like a lamprey before an armored warrior engaged the locking mechanism.

With a hiss of depressurization, the door opened, and the first whiff of Rendian air swirled into the cabin. It smelled fresh, and after a month of recycled spaceship air, Adriana took a deep breath, savoring it. The Rendians had assured the human scientists back on Earth that the Rendian atmosphere had a nearly identical composition to Earth's, which was the only way this mission could progress at all. It contained zero-point-two percent more oxygen, and far less carbon dioxide, which might even be beneficial to the humans.

The tube leading to the terminal was empty, a narrow tunnel lit by low bluish bulbs.

"Helmets on." The captain's command jerked Adriana from her thoughts.

The Rendians donned the last of their protective gear and heaved long spears made of the same light metal as the ship. Adriana had no idea what it was, but the two SEALs were watching the weapons with speculative expressions, probably thinking they should get their hands on a pair of them.

The lieutenant and three others stepped up next to the captain, and they advanced into the tunnel. The rest of the crew spaced themselves around the door and formed a sort of alien shield in front of the human delegation. Adriana knew they were acting under his orders, but she was grateful their protection was evidently part of the plan.

Seconds ticked by while everyone held their breaths, and then a voice croaked through the speakers, startling them all.

"*All passengers must disembark. All passengers must disembark.*"

Adriana exchanged a worried glance with Mika, but since their protectors were advancing down the corridor, the humans moved forward as well.

Moments later, they passed through the tube into a large hall—where a unit of soldiers waited for them, weapons drawn and leveled right at them.

4

Taron

HE'D BEEN GONE six months. Six months, and everything on Rendu had gone to shit.

The welcoming committee of soldiers were under orders to detain the humans in the hangar, and he had to fight the impulse to stab their sergeant through the eye and keep Adriana by his side. He could take them on, all of them, if they tried to touch her. As it was, he motioned for Lieutenant Anilla to remain with them, along with the rest of his crew, and followed the soldiers out into the cold.

The regent wanted to speak to him, they'd said, and formed a spiky circle of spears around him. Clearly, someone had informed them of his less than sanguine temper.

The frigid morning air was a welcome slap in the face. After Earth's pollution, Rendian air was almost sweet in his lungs, and his mind settled despite his fury. Earth had been nothing like he'd expected—beautiful but overrun by humans, who were so disrespectful of their own planet they were on the verge of destroying it completely.

He'd been half ready to call off the diplomatic mission; what good could a bunch of humans do on Rendu? And then he'd met the members of the research team, who were interested in *learning* from Rendians, it seemed, and didn't share the same attitude toward nature as the rest of their feeble species. And when he saw Dr. Adriana Ribeiro for the first time, the world slammed to a halt around him, and a fierce want gripped him in its claws. He would have done *anything* to bring her with him. If she hadn't been a part of the team, he suspected he might have kidnapped her and hid her in his cabin, keeping her all to himself.

Rolling his shoulders, Taron tried to convince himself she would be safe. That he would *not* return to find her and the rest of the humans dead and cold. The armed soldiers left him with no choice but to follow, and he understood his crew and the human delegation were hostages to ensure his good behavior.

Later, he would arrange a proper guard for the duration of her stay—by someone other than him—but right now, he needed to focus on the more immediate problem.

He wanted to ask after his brothers, but showing worry would look weak to these strangers. He knew none of them, which was odd despite his long absences. These weren't the royal guard, but some private force the regent must have cobbled together from his personal arsenal.

They entered the fortress by a side gate, which meant the regent didn't want to parade him through the streets. Having one of the late king's cousins dragged across town like a criminal might raise some eyebrows. Every piece of information was valuable in situations like this. The moment they stepped inside the palace, the formation these fools were holding no longer made sense. Built to withstand a siege, the palace had narrow corridors in which only two or three men could walk abreast. The nervous glances exchanged between the enemy soldiers told him they realized their disadvantage—their numbers would mean nothing on such a battleground.

They entered the throne room with little fanfare; what used to be a place of lively chatter and a hundred business deals being struck between members of the court was now an echoing chamber with only a handful of people milling at the far end.

Taron's gaze immediately zeroed in on his two brothers, standing at attention on the left. They were unarmed, which was telling enough since Lhett was the General of the Rendian army. It seemed like there was no end to the changes that occurred during his absence. He glanced at his brother's uniform—and shock coursed through him at the lack of Lhett's insignia. He'd been stripped of his rank?

Taron tried to meet his brothers' eyes, but they both stared ahead, resolute in their complete silence.

But they were alive and, as far as he could tell, unharmed. Taron didn't let himself be distracted by them; he was more interested in the man who'd caused all this.

Yaroh ad Gilmar, the former Chief of Commerce, was sitting on the throne. Next to him stood Zeema ad Luiten, the rightful Queen of Rendu, a girl two winters shy of majority. Her face was bone-white but composed despite the recent loss of her brother. If Taron didn't know his young cousin as well as he did, he might have missed the slight tremble of her hands as she gazed at him.

He wanted to murder Gilmar just for putting that look on Zeema's face. His brothers' inaction made no sense until he noticed the collar around her neck—made of the same metal as their spears and electronic wrist cuffs, it looked like a piece of ornate jewelry. Not many people knew it would short-circuit her brain at a press of a button.

Taron whipped his gaze back at the regent, and the man's smirk told him where that button was located.

"Welcome home, Soldier." The regent's voice rang out through the hall.

"It's Captain. And this place feels a lot less like a home today."

Movement to the left caught his attention, and he realized it was Kol, shaking his head slightly. Was his brother warning him not to talk back?

Gilmar's voice turned steely. "You have been stripped of your rank, effective immediately. Your only task from now on will be to ensure that the delegation of human scientists you just brought to our planet doesn't ruin the commercial development I've been planning for months. Their movements and actions must be contained to the capital."

Taron's mind reeled at his words, and he moved closer. "What? On what grounds? There's no precedent—"

The regent's guards stepped forward, their spears ready, but their master just waved them off.

"I don't need precedent. I thought you understood how this worked. The Galactic Trade Association will be monitoring the reports coming from the human scientists, and I don't want a whiff of what's happened here to reach them. It would hurt our trading rights, and I haven't worked like a slave for the past decade to have these warm-blooded morons fuck it all up." He straightened in the throne, gripping the armrests, and seemed to forcefully calm himself.

"The three of you will be the most motivated to follow my orders because of your cousin here."

Reaching out, Gilmar patted Zeema on the shoulder, and she flinched almost imperceptibly before flushing blue. Tears gathered in the corners of her eyes, and Taron wished he could give her his strength, his years of experience in hiding emotions. She was just a young woman who'd lost her closest family member, and by the looks of it, she hadn't even been allowed to mourn him properly. He had no idea whether they'd even held the royal funeral yet.

"You will report to duty immediately and take rooms in the same palace wing as the human delegation. You will eat, sleep, and breathe with them until the moment it's acceptable for us to make up some excuse and pack them back on that space junk of yours. Is that understood?"

"Yes."

"You will address me as Your Highness. I *am* the regent."

Gilmar was doing this purely out of spite, Taron knew, but the words still caught in his throat. "Yes, Your Highness."

With a last glance at Zeema, he turned to leave, his brothers falling into step behind him. As soon as they cleared the threshold of the first corridor, he faced them, but to his surprise, they each grabbed one of his arms and marched him out of the palace. Only when they were walking across the white plain toward the sky port did they speak.

"He poisoned the king," Kol told him. "And half the fucking Cabinet. The rest of the court is too scared to die—or to cause Zeema's death—to put up any resistance."

"So we're just doing what he asked?" Taron's voice

came out more sharply than he'd intended, but this was madness.

"Did you not see the collar Zeema is wearing?" Lhett stopped in the middle of the field, his jaw tight, his short white hair messy as though he'd run his fingers through it.

"I did, but he wouldn't—" Taron started to say.

But Lhett cut him off. "I made the mistake of going after Gilmar the moment we found out what had happened. He had the collar rigged so the electroshock is scalable. She screamed for hours." His brother's voice broke on that last word, and Taron gripped his shoulder, too appalled to speak.

"He's not stupid." Kol stared into the distance, where a snowstorm gathered around the high mountain peaks. "He left her alive and assumed the position of the regent as the oldest surviving member of the Cabinet. If he'd killed her, he would have had to go through us before he could make a serious claim on the throne."

Kol was right, of course. The line to the throne was clear, and while none of them had ever expected to take the position, the possibility had always been there.

Taron didn't want the fucking throne. He wanted his older cousin alive and well and his position as captain reinstated. He had a strong feeling that Zeema, almost two decades her brother's junior, had never had any aspirations for the throne either. She'd been more of a scholar than an authority figure, and she wasn't suited for the secretive life of intrigue that came with ruling the country.

But for now, at least, it seemed they would all have to play by the regent's rules. He lengthened his stride to reach Adriana as fast as possible. There was no guarantee that Gilmar hadn't done something nasty to the humans already.

"Fine," he said. "We'll lay low for now and see what can be done."

"What are the humans like?" Kol asked as they sped toward the sky port, crossing the barren, icy land that stretched from the capital's outer walls.

Taron thought for a moment, the image of Adriana clear in his mind. "Warm. Curious." He paused before admitting, "Stunning."

At his brothers' silence, he glanced back. Lhett was frowning, but Kol's knowing grin had him wishing he could punch something. Or someone. "What?"

"An affair with a human would complicate everything even further," Lhett said, ever the pragmatic.

"But it would be so much fun," Kol returned. "And look at him, he's already halfway gone."

Taron scowled at them. "It won't be a problem. I'm not halfway anything."

"Sure, keep telling yourself that."

5

Adriana

"OH MY, there's three of them."

At her friend Hanne's comment, Adriana put down her tablet and stared at the entrance to their prison. In truth, it was only a windowless storage space at the airport, but it had certainly felt like a cell since guards were stationed at the door, silent and menacing, their spears humming with electricity.

But now Captain Naals and two other massive Rendians appeared at the door, dismissing the guards with nothing but a terse word.

The captain's gaze landed on her, and he made two steps in her direction before he stopped himself. She bit her lip; she had no idea what emotion inspired the dark look in his eyes. The hair on the back of her neck rose, and she shivered despite her protective gear.

He clenched his jaw and drew back his shoulders, then

addressed his crew members. "We're grounded for the fore-seeable future. Your new objective is to guard and help the human delegation. Go home tonight and report for duty at dawn tomorrow. We'll be stationed in the east wing of the palace."

There was some grumbling, but his dozen subordinates picked up their various belongings and disappeared through the door. Then the captain's attention was all on them.

"You've come to know my crew during the trip here, so the regent decided it would be easiest if they served as your protective detail."

"You still haven't told us what we need protection from," Ben called, voicing what they were discussing earlier.

"The elements, Doctor Maas," the captain answered. "And your own curiosity. You wouldn't be the first visitor to this planet to wander off in pursuit of a herd of rica, only to end up frozen when an ice storm rolls in." His gaze swept over them, his brow furrowed. "We're not here to impede your investigations but to help you stay alive."

Adriana narrowed her eyes at him. There was more he wasn't telling them, she was sure of it. Why else would they be worried and armed when they disembarked from the spaceship? What were they going to shoot at—the wind? But as soon as she opened her mouth, he sent her a glare so severe, she decided to bide her time. Nothing good would come of her questioning his authority. She'd have to get answers...in private.

The warrior on Taron's left, short-haired and scarred, was introduced as Lhett, while the one on his right, whose long white hair was unbound, was Kol. Adriana was fairly sure they were brothers, which was just unfair. Some people were blessed with incredible genes even on other planets. Taron glared at her some more before turning away.

Kol caught her gaze from across the room, and when Taron launched into another list of orders, he strode right up to her, bowed deeply, and took her hand to press a kiss to her knuckles. His hands were cold, like all Rendians', but the contact wasn't unpleasant.

"Kol ad Naals, at your service."

His light-blue eyes sparkled at her, and Adriana thought she heard Mika catch her breath from beside her.

"Um, hi!" Adriana squeaked. "I'm Adriana. That is, Dr. Adriana Ribeiro."

"And what part of our humble planet will you be exploring?"

He straightened but didn't release her hand, and a blush crept over her cheeks.

"Oh, you're turning red!" Kol grinned, then stroked the back of his fingers over her cheek. "And you were right, brother, they're warm all over."

"I'm an extraterrestrial anthropologist," she answered, trying not to sound breathless. These Rendian warriors sure had a mighty presence. "So I'm interested—"

"Get your hands off her."

Taron was suddenly standing there, his normally pale face an interesting shade of midnight blue, his eyes dark as sapphires. Adriana stared at him, mesmerized. He was beautiful and unearthly, his impressive muscles locked tight as he pulled his brother away from her.

He put himself between her and Kol, who was now laughing, his hands raised in surrender, and Adriana was left to stare at Taron's broad, spiky back, still encased in that strange armor. She raised a finger and caressed one of the ridged bones that protruded from between the shoulder blades, both to see what the armor would feel like against her skin and to annoy him. The effect was similar to fish scales, if fish were encased in ultra-thin metal.

He shrugged as though to remove a fly from his back—Adriana supposed he barely felt her touch through the armor—but didn't turn to look at her.

"Stand down, Taron." Lhett appeared next to Kol, his expression unimpressed. "You know he's only playing with you."

At Hanne's nudge and wink, Adriana had to wonder: Would Taron have reacted the same if Kol had kissed Mika's hand? It was a slippery slope, following this line of thought. She could be imagining that his attention was specifically reserved for her.

And she couldn't afford to mess up this mission, not when so much depended on it when she returned to Earth. So she stepped back, even though she wanted to keep touching Taron, to run her palms all over his hard body. His strong arms had featured in some incredibly inappropriate fantasies she'd had in the privacy of her cabin on his space-ship. It had felt almost indecent, since the entire ship belonged to him, but his kiss had left her wanting, yearning, and she'd been faced with the option of either self-combusting or taking the edge off that lust herself.

Swallowing a lump of regret, she reminded herself she was the first anthropologist in history to have the opportunity to study a non-human civilization. The first to observe their societal patterns and traditions.

She'd still been an undergrad student when Rendians landed on Earth more than five years ago. Their discovery of Earth had been a fluke, a cosmic coincidence that had thrust Earth into a new era. The Chinese had launched a deep space probe similar to the *Voyager* spacecraft in 2002, and it had entered interstellar space, passing out of the solar system, by the end of 2013. The probe lost all contact with Earth before long and was promptly forgotten by most people, until a shiny, massive spaceship appeared over Greenland.

The aliens had found the space probe and thought it had gotten lost, so they set out to return it. Interested in exploring a planet that had an atmosphere with a composition similar to theirs, they landed on the snowy island because it most closely resembled their home planet.

Their arrival caused mass panic—and mass adoration, since they were unfairly stunning as a race. Adriana applied for an internship with the newly established Extraterrestrial Ministry of the United States the moment the position opened, and later for the coveted option to be a member of this pioneering team.

She hadn't even stopped to think about it—she'd filled the forms out, praying for a chance to travel into space. And when she'd been accepted, she'd known, deep inside, that it had been the right decision. She'd been born to do this. It would be enough to make her entire career on Earth.

It *might* just be enough to impress her parents. But she wasn't so sure about that. They'd wanted her to become a doctor—the *real* kind, as they'd often told her, even after she'd aced her own post-grad studies in record time—and their opinion of her profession hadn't changed. She doubted it ever would. If they weren't proud of their daughter for being among the first humans to experience interstellar travel, nothing could shake them from their set ways.

She suspected even her straightlaced mother might have found something to admire among these gorgeous aliens, though.

Kol retreated to a respectable distance, and Taron

slowly lost his blue flush. His demeanor didn't change—his voice was barely more than a growl when he forced out through clenched teeth, "Gather your personal luggage. Your gear will be delivered into the hall that will serve as your office space." With that, he turned away and stalked to the door.

Adriana let out a breath she wasn't aware she'd been holding. They'd only been on Rendu for two hours, and already tensions were rising high. It wouldn't do, not if their mission was to be a success.

"I don't really care where our gear goes, as long as I get some dinner," she said, loud enough to be heard over the low murmur of her crewmates. Several people snorted, and Kol sent her an appraising look, as though he knew exactly that she was trying to diffuse the situation.

"You won't go hungry, Dr. Ribeiro," he promised, then inclined his head toward the door. "You'd better follow him, though. He'll be even more unbearable if we fail to obey his orders."

Adriana was conscious of how her colleagues fell silent the moment they stepped outside the sky port's door. They'd all bundled up in heavy winter gear, so at least she wasn't the only one who resembled a bread roll anymore. The air was biting cold, finding cracks between layers of clothing, stinging her eyes, her cheeks, her wrists, where hastily pulled-on gloves failed to insulate her skin.

But it didn't matter. Because she was standing on a freaking alien planet, watching a purple moon that hung low in the sky, impossibly large against the icy peaks of the mountain range. It was completely different from Earth and unbelievably beautiful.

A small sob escaped her, and she covered her mouth with her mitten, but Taron was there in a second, taking her chin and turning her face up to him. The rest of the crew moved on, herded by Taron's brothers, and it seemed to her that they were the only creatures on this desolate world.

"Don't be sad," he murmured, swiping a cold thumb over her cheek with such tenderness, something squeezed inside her.

She nodded, sniffling, and pressed her lips together to compose herself.

"It takes a while to get used to," he continued. "We'll get some food in you, then you can rest, and everything will be better by tomorrow."

She managed a weak smile. "Is that a promise?"

How he stared at her...Adriana had never experienced such intensity in a man, and she had no idea how she would navigate this complicated, inter-species relationship with him. If what they had could even be classified as a relationship.

His gaze roamed over her face, as though he was trying to memorize every detail. Then he lowered his cool lips and pressed a hard, quick kiss on her mouth, leaving her breathless. He released her immediately, robbing her of a chance to react, to return the kiss like she wanted to.

He didn't look away from her as he replied, "It's a promise."

6

Adriana

THAT KISS WOULD BE BURNED into her memory for an eternity, no matter how quick it was. One does not simply forget her first...or second kiss with an alien.

It took every ounce of her will to stop herself from pulling him into her new room after he escorted her there. But her crew members were milling around the corridor, exclaiming over the luxurious apartments they'd been assigned, and she hadn't wanted them to know just how infatuated she was with Captain Naals. With Taron.

Whenever he appeared in her dreams, he asked her to call him by his name.

Adriana swallowed, ruthlessly suppressing that memory before one of the Rendian crew in the big dining hall noticed her flush. They seemed to delight in making humans blush—though she had to admit her colleagues were just as fascinated by their hosts.

Ben, the doctor responsible for keeping the human crew members healthy, had confided in her during their interstellar flight, that he'd tried getting a blood sample from a Rendian in order to study it. "They, uh, weren't very keen on that idea," the tall Dutch doctor had said, scratching his short blond hair.

Taking a bowl of steaming soup from a man in a gray uniform, Adriana sat at one of the unoccupied tables in the mess hall, content to be alone with her thoughts at the moment. She'd wondered what it would be like to have sex with a Rendian, of course. *Fine*, not just any Rendian but one specific soldier, muscular and taller than her by a full head. Was all of his body as cold as his hands, his lips? A shudder ran through her at the thought of how amazing it would be to have his long, hard—

"Good morning."

Adriana squeaked and whirled around, startled to find Taron and his brothers just a couple of steps behind her. She'd never been more grateful that these particular extraterrestrials didn't have mind reading abilities. Luckily, her reaction was swallowed by a chorus of *Hellos* from the rest of the people.

Taron strode to the center of the room and said, "Since each of you has their own area of expertise, we thought it would be easiest if personal guides were assigned to you. That way, you'll be able to pursue your own investigations without waiting for other crew members to finish their own work."

Murmurs of assent rippled through the hall. Then Mika's bright voice piped up, "I want *him*."

They all turned to see where she was pointing, and Adriana saw, to her surprise, that Kol had flushed a light blue at all the extra attention.

Taron even cracked a smile. "That can be arranged. Your assigned guides will find you soon."

Adriana knew it was foolish to hope that he'd assign himself to her, and slurped up some of the delicious noodles that floated in her soup. Breakfast choices were different from what she was used to, but the food was superb.

When he walked over to the table where the two SEALs were sharing something that looked like an entire mutton leg, she swallowed a sigh. It was probably better that she got matched with someone else. Taron's people skills were abominable, and he'd only growl at the Rendian locals she was supposed to be studying. Her guide should probably be someone nice and personable.

A shadow fell across her table, and then Taron sat on the bench next to her. "Hello," he murmured, low enough that she had to lean closer to hear him. Their thighs touched, and the scent of him, fresh and minty, invaded her senses.

"You picked me?" She fought the grin that threatened to curl her lips.

"We drew lots," he answered but glanced away from her when she narrowed her eyes at him. Then he took hold of her hand under the table and entwined his larger fingers with hers, squeezing lightly.

The touch sent shivers through her body, and a pool of warmth ignited deep inside her. She bit back a moan as he pressed the pad of each finger, his strong hands keeping her captive in that private moment.

Adriana looked up, suddenly conscious they were sitting in full view of the others, but Taron's voice pulled her back into the spell. "Nobody is watching us."

And yet anyone could notice at any moment, and the thrill of the thought was delicious. Adriana's nipples tightened, and she was grateful her bra hid the worst of her reaction. But Taron turned a faint blue, clearly noticing, and he dropped her hand suddenly, placing it on her knee instead.

She glanced into his lap, curious to see if his tight uniform showed any sign of his excitement. That was when she noticed he wasn't wearing his usual form-fitting wonder of clothing design that had her wishing she could tear it off him with her teeth, but rather a set of what she supposed were Rendian civilian clothes. The pants were made of some dark, supple leather, and his pullover resembled cashmere. Adriana wanted to snuggle in close to see if it was as soft as it seemed, but that would be a pretty big clue for everyone in the room that she'd developed an obsession with Taron ad Naals.

She shook herself from the daydream and forced her mind back on the task that had brought her to Rendu in the first place: observing and exploring their society.

"So you're going to be my guide?" she asked.

Taron looked pained, his jaw clenching and unclenching before he nodded. "I couldn't let anyone else take care of you."

This would have made her bristle—she didn't need anyone *taking care* of her—but his expression was so earnest, she suspected this confession had cost him a lot. And if she was being perfectly honest...

"I'm glad you picked me," she whispered. "But I'm not sure how I'll be able to concentrate with you around. This is highly unprofessional." What she didn't add was that she'd been just a little heartbroken when he'd cut her off after their first kiss. She didn't want her heart bruised if he suddenly decided he didn't want her anymore.

"I'll keep my hands to myself."

He moved a foot to the left, and Adriana mourned the space between them.

"Right." She swallowed a lump of something that felt suspiciously like regret.

He looked around the room, where Rendians were chatting with humans, and Adriana tried to guess what was going on inside his head. Rendians had had contact with multiple other species in the universe, so this couldn't possibly be as weird for him as it was for her. She searched for her friends and realized Mika had gotten her wish—Kol was leading her from the hall, already busy explaining something to her. To her surprise, mild-mannered Hanne seemed to be having a heated argument with Lhett, who was bright blue in the face and gesticulating wildly.

Adriana got up to see if she could help resolve the argument, but Taron placed a hand on her shoulder, removing it immediately after. "Wait. If they're going to spend the next three months together, they need to fight their own battles."

He was likely right, so she sat and watched nervously as Hanne threw her arms up and strode out of the room, and Lhett stalked behind her, muttering something under his breath.

"She's safe with him, though, right?" Adriana asked, eyeing the scarred alien's retreating back.

"I trust him with my life," Taron replied.

And weirdly enough, that was all she needed to hear. When had she come to trust Captain Naals so completely?

"What do you want to do today?" he asked, interrupting her thoughts.

"Oh, right! I thought you could show me around the city," she said. "I need to get a sense of the place, see where people shop, where they pray, and so on."

"I can do that." He motioned at her soup bowl. "Do you

want any more? You'll need the energy in the cold. Vissnae tentacles are hardly filling."

Adriana stared into her bowl, where a lone noodle swam in the remaining broth. *Tentacles?*

Sampling a culture's food was a good way of getting to know its people, but she usually liked knowing what she was eating. Swallowing, she got up and carried her bowl back to the serving table. "I'm good, thanks," she told Taron, deciding to search for something like bagels for her next meal if at all possible.

He followed her to her room, where he watched her put on her winter clothes with such intensity, she was flushed red by the time she finished—and not from overheating, though the rooms were incredibly warm given the outside temperatures.

Then he pinched the pompom on top of her raspberry-pink woolen beanie, and grinned at her, his white teeth flashing against pale-blue skin, and her heart skipped a beat. Damn, but the man was gorgeous. She hadn't seen many Rendians apart from his crew and the emissaries who had visited Earth, but he was beautiful even by their standards. His high forehead, a straight, flat nose, and slightly pointed, high-set ears should have made him look too strange to her. But she couldn't stop staring at him: his wide, clear blue eyes held so much intelligence, and his firm, sensuous lips promised so much pleasure.

She mentally gave herself a firm kick in the butt. This was not the time to daydream about Taron.

"How is the palace heated?" she asked as they strode out into the corridor, more to redirect his focus from herself than from actual curiosity. Their resident engineer, Jean, would be more interested in stuff like that.

But Taron seemed pleased she'd asked. "Thermal energy," he explained. "Most of the land around here is volcanic, though we haven't had an eruption in centuries. But the thermal springs here allow for central heating and our greenhouses. It's where we grow most of our plant-based food."

"That's incredible," she said, intrigued. Their geologist, Svetlana, would have a blast exploring the planet. "Will you show me that as well?"

He laughed, the sound so rich and wonderful, she stared at him, half forgetting what they were talking about.

"We have a lot of time, Earthling," he said. "We don't have to do everything today."

She found herself smiling back. "No, of course not. But I should probably start making a list of things I want to see and do."

They strode out into the open, but only for a short walk across a large, empty square. Her cheeks pinched with cold, and she reminded herself to breathe through her nose to avoid searing her lungs with the frigid air. Soon, they ducked through a thick set of doors into a covered marketplace, and it immediately became clear to Adriana that most of Rendian life happened in such great, cramped spaces because the outside world was just too hostile.

What also stood out immediately was her. In her lime-green parka, she was like a colorful tropical fish in a tank full of herring.

The native population wore wool in cool shades of white and gray that fit their pale-blue skin well. Their clothes were simply cut and elegant, showcasing their long limbs and powerful muscles. Women and men alike were dressed in pants, rather than skirts, and seemed to favor practicality and warmth over frills and decorations. Adriana's dark hair and brown skin were very noticeable, but she'd be able to blend in better if she picked Rendian clothes. There was no way she'd be able to observe the society as it was if everyone was too busy staring at her.

Taron must have noticed everyone's attention as well, because he glued himself to her side and frowned so fiercely, Adriana would have scuttled away if it wasn't for her protection. When an older man jostled her shoulder in the crowd, and she nearly went flying from the impact, he simply tucked her into his side, his arm around her shoulder.

Oh my. It didn't help with people staring at them, that was for sure. Noticing how people nodded at Taron, almost reverently, and how many greetings he had to return, she poked his side so he leaned in closer.

"Who are you?" she asked.

"No one of consequence," he murmured in her ear, his cool lips brushing her skin. "Not anymore."

As he pulled her forward, she added that cryptic remark to the list of things she had to investigate. But a crowded market was hardly a place for a personal interrogation of the man whose secrets she wanted to learn.

They stepped into a large circular hall, its domed ceiling made of some sort of glass that allowed in light but not the cold. Voices of hundreds of aliens echoed through the space, bargains being struck, arguments breaking out over wares from all over the universe. Adriana stopped, frozen in her tracks, and stared.

Apart from the native Rendians, numerous other races rushed around them, peddling their exotic goods or buying big bales of wool, their statures too varied and colorful for comprehension. An alien with three heads and a tall, lithe body that flowed into a mustard-yellow tail served steaming cups of beverages to a pod of pink blob-like creatures that extended suckers to slurp up their drinks. A man—or at least Adriana assumed he was a man, though it was entirely possible his race didn't even have sexes, let alone genders—carried a cage of red chickens whose beaks were filled with razor-sharp teeth. A silky-furred fox the size of a wolfhound snuck through the crowd, a chain of sausages dangling from its jaws.

"Pinch me," she whispered. Taron chuckled at her side. "This is incredible. This..." She paused, trying to find the right words. "From what you told us, I knew there were other planets with sentient life forms, but this..."

"This is just a fraction of them all," he finished for her. "Will you travel to other planets once you're finished on Rendu?"

There was something in his expression, a clenching of his jaw, a tightness around his eyes. Adriana slipped an arm around his waist, feeling the strength of his muscles when she gave him a short, hard squeeze.

"There's enough to learn on Rendu to last a lifetime."

His smile was sad as he replied, "But you only have three months."

Her answering grin was a little forced, a little bitter. "Let's not waste any time then."

Taron held her gaze for a moment, then nodded and took her hand, holding her fingers gently in his much larger palm. "Follow me."

"Where are you taking me?"

He didn't slow down but merely threw a smirk over his shoulder. "Just trust me."

Adriana held on and put her faith in an alien man, knowing deep down she'd already given away a part of herself that would never be returning to Earth with her.

7

Taron

VINSHA'S SHOP was one that Princess Zeema had always visited when she had need of good quality, plain clothes that allowed her to mingle with her brother's subjects. Or she had, before this entire thing blew up. Now these people were *her* subjects, even though she was currently nothing but a puppet under Gilmar's control.

That didn't change the fact that Vinsha supplied the capital with the best clothes money could buy. And though his family's accounts had been frozen, Taron still had enough loose coin to be able to buy his warm-blooded protégée an outfit that would allow her to blend in better.

He knew it was only his presence keeping the men—and probably some women—away from her today; he'd seen their covetous glances. Humans were a novelty on Rendu, and with Adriana's looks, she would likely receive several courting offers before the day was over. The thought had his blood boiling, and he tugged her closer, putting his arm around her to keep her safe. Having her near eased his mind, calmed the incessant buzz of the crowd. He couldn't pinpoint the sensation, but her presence soothed an itch he'd never known existed.

It helped that she didn't seem to mind, sticking close to him and even leaning on him whenever the crowd became too dense and her short stature put her at a disadvantage compared to his taller race.

They reached Vinsha's shop without incident, but Taron was glad to have the door close behind them. They plunged into silence only broken by the gentle music piping through hidden speakers, which added a layer of calm to the shopping experience.

The owner herself approached them, raising her eyebrows a fraction at the sight of Adriana but otherwise keeping a pleasant smile on her face. A true merchant, Vinsha knew not to insult a client by gawking.

"If it isn't my favorite prince," she crooned.

Taron closed his eyes for a moment. He felt Adriana's curious stare, but this wasn't the time or the place. "Hello, Vinsha," he said.

The older woman pursed her lips, reading his reluctance to indulge in small talk. "Hmm. What can I help you with today?"

She looked at Adriana then, and the human simply shrugged, her gaze taking in the racks of clothing.

"We need a full outfit for Dr. Ribeiro," he said. "Blending in is, ah, crucial for her assignment, and..." He trailed off, pointing helplessly at Adriana's green coat and red hat.

"Hey," she said, her hands on her hips. "I'll have you know this is the finest Arctic gear Earth has to offer."

"Mm," Vinsha agreed, "but perhaps not the most inconspicuous." She took Adriana's hand, and if her touch was a little too long—she was likely as amazed at Adriana's warmth as Taron had been—she didn't let the surprise show on her face.

"True," Adriana laughed.

Taron realized with some relief that she wasn't affronted.

Vinsha turned on her heel and strode between the shelves like a general surveying her armies. "You'll be more susceptible to cold, yes? Let's look at some of these shirts, they're lined with mantora fur..."

Taron kept quiet and helped the women by carrying the increasingly large pile of clothes Vinsha insisted Adriana should wear. They spoke the same language despite having been born on planets light-years apart.

When they completed a circuit of the shop, Vinsha showed Adriana to a changing area in the back. Just as she was urging her to shout if any of the garments proved to be the wrong size, the bell above the shop's door chimed quietly, announcing the arrival of another customer.

"Will you be all right here?" Vinsha asked.

Adriana waved her off with assurances that Taron would help if needed.

As soon as the shopkeeper left, Adriana looked him in the eyes. "Sorry for forcing you to carry my stuff around. I know this isn't what you signed up for. If you want, you can go do something else. I'll be fine on my own."

"I'm your guard," he said. "I'm not supposed to leave your side."

"I could have sworn you said 'guide,' not 'guard' this morning," she replied with a cheeky smile that had him wishing he could kiss her to teach her not to make fun of him.

Instead, he lifted an eyebrow, settling against the wall opposite the stall. "I'm at your service, Dr. Ribeiro," he murmured and had the pleasure of seeing her flush prettily before she disappeared behind the curtain.

That was when the torture began. He hadn't considered the most obvious part of trying on clothes: she had to take hers off in order to try on the new ones. One garment after the other landed on the curtain rail, and Taron gritted his teeth, readjusting himself in his pants, thankful for their snug fit and the cover of his long jacket.

Adriana's mutters from the inside were just quiet enough to be unintelligible, but the soft gasp of delight prompted him to take a step closer to the cabin, an involuntary move that would have ended with him ripping away the curtain if she hadn't opened it herself.

"What do you think?"

She stepped out, twirling, her generous hips wrapped in the finest rica leather. He knew it would be soft, supple enough to sleep in if need be. His fingers itched to touch, and he clasped his hands behind his back instead.

The sweater was at least a size too big for her, though, the sleeves reaching her fingertips. "Keep the pants, and I'll bring you a smaller pullover," he grunted, turning on his heel and stalking back into the shop before he grabbed her and did something really stupid, like strip that leather from her and take her against the wall of Vinsha's shop.

He returned to the stall, thinking he had himself back under control, although he'd have to schedule some alone time in his bath after the day was over.

He thrust his hand through the gap between the wall and the curtain, but his sleeve snagged the fabric and pulled it open just enough to allow him a peek inside—lucky coincidence, perhaps, but it was enough to crumble his resistance to dust.

He caught Adriana's gaze in the mirror; a beat passed, and then he gave in to the temptation and lowered his gaze, swiping down her body. Transfixed by her beauty, he wouldn't have been able to move if a comet was bearing down on the city at that moment.

She was still wearing those sinful leather pants, but the sweater was gone, with only a scrap of fabric covering her lush breasts. It was completely impractical, a sheer textile that wouldn't warm her at all, but it did spectacular things to her body, showing her dark nipples, already hard. Her brown skin shone golden under the shop's lights, her narrow waist flaring into hips he wanted to grip as he sank himself inside her hot body.

He dragged his gaze back to her face, aware he was flushing but too aroused to care. Prepared to apologize for the intrusion, he looked her in the eyes again but saw not an ounce of embarrassment in her gaze. No, this human held her head high and lifted an eyebrow in challenge.

She was *teasing* him. A wave of lust washed away the last of his objections. Taron didn't even glance over his shoulder before he slipped inside the stall, drawing the curtain closed.

He stepped up behind her, until her soft body molded to his, warming him even through his layer of clothes. Bringing his hands around her, he gently cupped her breasts, and the catch in her breathing hit him like a punch to the gut. She didn't look away from him, her dark eyes challenging him, a faint smile curving her plump lips while her breathing quickened.

"Don't make a sound," he whispered into her ear, and

close as he was, he felt a tremor run through her body, but she nodded, leaning her head against his chest.

He traced the lines of her body, watching the contrast of his pale skin on hers, loving the silky skin that indented under his fingertips. And the warmth, ah, the warmth of her was addictive. When he'd kissed her before, he'd sensed her body's reaction to him, the incremental change in temperature that signaled to him just how aroused she was. And now...

She burned, her skin almost hot to the touch, her breath tickling his neck as she turned her face to him.

He couldn't resist; he slipped his palms down her soft belly, circling her navel with one finger, then traced the waistband of those leather pants that would haunt his dreams for the rest of his life.

"Look at yourself," he muttered, and she obeyed, following the trail of his fingers in the mirror.

He undid the laces in the front, then slipped a hand inside her underwear, and groaned when he touched the soft curls between her legs. And then he touched the core of her, the little button of nerves that had her gasping, slippery from her arousal. He rolled his finger over it, thanking his ancestors that human anatomy didn't differ from the Rendian in that aspect.

She moaned, and he put his other hand over her mouth. "Shhh."

Even though she nodded, he didn't let go. This was the most erotic sight he'd ever seen. Flick after slow flick, he worked her, then reached lower to slide a finger inside her wet heat.

He pressed his face to the top of her head, too close to coming at the thought of sinking his cock into that warmth.

When he stilled his finger, she rocked her hips, seeking contact, and he chuckled against her hair.

She glowered at him but couldn't speak because of his hand covering her mouth; instead of releasing her, he pushed two fingers inside her again, whispering, "Is this what you want?"

A shudder racked her small frame, and she leaned more heavily on him, circling her hips with every stroke. Her breaths came faster, and in the mirror, he saw her eyelids flutter shut. "No," he said, "see how gorgeous you are. Watch as I make you fall apart."

But when she opened her eyes, she didn't look at where his fingers were buried deep inside her, stroking her again and again. She met his gaze instead, and the heat there almost brought him to the edge, his cock so hard against her ass. He rocked his hips, unable to stop himself.

With another deep, slow slide of his fingers, she shattered in his arms. She threw her arms out, catching herself on the mirror, her palms leaving sweaty marks on the glass, and he muffled the worst of her moans with his palm. He kissed the back of her neck, tasting salt on her skin, then licked her, wishing they were in his rooms where he could pull those pants down her legs and plunge into her from behind.

He let her go when he was sure she could stand, and leaned back against the wall, fighting to get his breathing under control. After a moment, she lifted her head, meeting his gaze again in the mirror.

"What the hell was that?" she whispered.

He shrugged. "I didn't want to waste any more time." *And you looked so beautiful, I couldn't resist.*

Turning toward him, she swiped her gaze down his body, noticing his erection.

"Oh, you poor man." Her eyes sparkled as she stepped closer to him, pressing her hot palms on his chest, exploring his body through his clothes. "You seem to be suffering."

He glanced at the curtain, aware that Vinsha could return at any moment. He didn't think the shopkeeper would interrupt, but he also didn't want rumors spreading that Taron ad Naals fucked humans in public.

But this little human already had his pants open, she was reaching inside before he had a chance to object, and the moment her warm, small fingers closed around his cock, all rational thought fled his brain.

"Shhh." There was a definite smirk on her face when he let out a groan, so he kissed her, invaded her mouth, and poured all the lust he had into that kiss, wanting to wipe that smug look off her face. The plan backfired; she sucked on his tongue and pumped his cock.

His hips moved on instinct, rocking into her hot fist. He didn't know how much time passed; he never wanted this to end. Adriana's eager, slick mouth was paradise. He caught her up against him, filled his hands with her ass, so sumptuous in the soft leather.

She swiped her thumb over his cock head and added a firm twist to every tug. *Sorceress.* She bewitched him, drove him crazy, made him forget all his plans and doubts...

"Adriana," he panted.

With a thud, he leaned back and clamped his jaw to keep from shouting out loud.

He came all over her fingers and stomach, shuddering, gasping at the strength of his explosion, grateful for the solid wall at his back that supported his weight. The world disappeared, that sense of calm descending over him, blocking out everything that wasn't Adriana.

She moaned at the sight of him, her pupils wide, and

Taron knew she was somehow close again, her body temperature spiking at the sight of his orgasm.

If they didn't leave now, Vinsha would have to close the shop for the day.

Then Adriana whispered, "It's so cold," and licked her fingers, *tasting* his come like it was honey. "Oh shit," she added, licking another finger, "this is incredible."

Taron grabbed her discarded thermal shirt and wiped her fingers and stomach. "Stop it."

She looked up at him, eyes wide, apprehension flitting over her face. "Am I not supposed to? I'm sorry, I didn't realize..."

He pushed her against the mirror and kissed her again, a raw, savage kiss that stole their breaths.

"If you don't stop, I'll take you right here. Fuck you until you're screaming my name, and I don't want anyone else hearing that." His voice was unrecognizable, a low rasp he forced through his teeth.

She wrapped her arms around his neck and kissed him back, molding her body to his. "I'm not sure I'd stop you," she murmured in his ear.

He laughed quietly, then stepped back. "You're going to need that sweater, you know. Your shirt is ruined."

She motioned at a small pile of clothes. "Those are the ones I want. I might need more later but I should be able to blend in better with them." She checked her reflection in the mirror and patted her black hair down, and gasped suddenly. "You gave me a hickey!"

He cocked his head to the side. "A what?"

Pointing to a purple bruise on the side of her neck, she said, "A love bite! You bit me. Ohh, Mika and Hanne will have a field day with this."

Taron didn't understand what she meant by that,

exactly, but for the most part, he liked seeing his mark on her skin. He felt a twinge of guilt at the sight and ran his fingertips lightly over the bruise. "Does it hurt?"

She turned in his arms. "No. But it won't go away for several days, and I'll have to wear a scarf to hide it. We better find one in the shop."

Grinning down at her—she was so *short*—he replied, "Or you could show it off and tell everyone how great I am."

"Very funny," she grumbled, then pushed him through the curtain. "Now get out, I need to get dressed."

Taron laced his pants quickly before turning back to the shop. From the other side, Vinsha gave him an amused look and winked. *Well, shit.* Their secret moment wasn't so secret after all. He glowered back at her, and she pressed her hand to her heart, then lifted a finger to point at the ceiling. A promise to keep their privacy, unspoken, perhaps, but no less binding.

He nodded, accepting her gift. Vinsha might become an ally yet. Ancestors knew he needed them these days.

Glancing back at the changing stall, he sighed when reality poured back in, forcing him to push away all thoughts of taking Adriana to his rooms—he didn't even have *rooms* anymore, just a single room in the same corridor as Adriana and the rest of his crew who were now designated guides to the human delegation. His family's house had been seized by the regent's forces, and sealed off, preventing them from accessing the well-stocked armory Lhett had compiled over the years.

He scrubbed his palm across his face. This was exactly the opposite of the regent's orders. If she got close to him, he would have a harder time keeping secrets from her, especially one as massive as the fact that the queen was being held hostage by a sociopath.

He'd have to stop all physical contact with Adriana. Protecting her would be harder without touching her, yet each touch brought that sense of peace, addictive and enticing, making him want more. It would be better if he kept his word to her and kept his hands to himself.

For a brief moment, he even thought about switching places with one of his brothers or his crew. Then Adriana stepped from behind the curtain, her arms full of clothing, and gave him the most brilliant smile, her beautiful face shining just for him. As he stepped forward to relieve her of her burden, he knew he wouldn't be able to let her go. Certainly not now, maybe not ever. Which was a problem, because in just three months, she'd be leaving this planet for good.

8

Adriana

FOR THE NEXT WEEK, Taron showed her his city. The pride that shone in his eyes whenever she gasped at a particularly beautiful building told her he loved his home, and she had to wonder why he chose to leave it for months at a time as a spaceship captain. She'd never felt such happiness when she walked the streets of Orlando, where she'd grown up, or even Nuuk, the largest town in Greenland, where she'd spent the better part of the past two years preparing for the mission. Taron was clearly invested in the life of the capital, and she'd asked about it, remembering Vinsha's strange comment about him being a prince.

"The queen is my cousin on my mother's side," he'd explained quietly.

He fingered the fastenings of his wool coat, though Adriana wasn't certain he was aware of it.

"So you're royalty?" She'd raised her eyebrows, trying to

wrap her head around the fact that a *prince* was escorting her around the city.

Taron inclined his head. "In a manner of speaking. Zeema has no other relatives. Lhett is the first in line for the throne until she marries and has children."

"Wow." Adriana pondered this for a moment. "She's so young to be queen."

She'd seen the composed young woman only once during their first week at the palace, passing through a corridor up ahead. She'd hoped to maybe gain access to an interview with her—it would be fascinating to hear how the young female monarch coped with the stress of her position and what her vision was for her planet.

Taron had mumbled something unintelligible and changed the subject, pointing at a colorful display of wares at a market stall.

He took her to schools and kindergartens, where she observed younglings learning from tablets that flashed with the strange, loopy symbols that made up the Rendian writing—more like Chinese characters than the Latin alphabet. There was music, God, such music that raised all the hairs on her neck, played on flute-like instruments while the chorus sang in clear, sonorous voices.

He showed her the burial pyres at the edge of the city, on the shore of the vast frozen sea that extended to the horizon. Rendians burned their dead and scattered their ashes to the wind, convinced their ancestors continued to roam the universe and watched over their descendants.

Their culture was as rich and varied as any Adriana had observed on Earth, and her heart ached at the thought of leaving—she could no more document all the intricacies of this society in three months than she could count the stars in the sky. She tried, though, hoping to do it justice by recording her notes in her journals and taking photos as unobtrusively as she could, both on film and with her digital camera, afraid one or the other might become damaged.

She was sitting on her bed, dressed in pajamas and ready to sleep, going through her plans for the next week, when a dull thud from the corridor broke her focus. Setting aside her notes on the remote mountain villages she'd found marked on a map of the continent, she tiptoed to the door and listened.

Taron's muffled voice filtered through, but it didn't seem like he was talking to anyone, just cursing, and then there was the telltale slide of his door shutting. Silence reigned, and Adriana chewed her lip, unsure of what to do.

Her guide-slash-guard had been perfectly civil these past days, taking her where she wanted to go, never complaining if she stayed to ask questions and take notes. But he hadn't touched her once beyond helping her stay upright in a crowd or guiding her over frozen patches of ground that threatened her ankles. He'd been a gentleman, in other words.

But the truth was, Adriana didn't want a gentleman. She wanted Taron from the spaceship, Taron from the clothes shop who had kissed her and made her come so hard, her legs still trembled a week after the fact. Every time she thought about those stolen minutes, about his words— they'd been half threat, half promise—she found herself growing wet, and had to fight a flush so he didn't comment on it.

Sometimes, she thought he sensed her arousal. He'd look at her, move a step closer, then clench his fists and retreat again. When he was with her, he grew a touch less grumpy, too, laughing at her lame jokes and making an effort to chat with the locals while she conducted her interviews. He'd helped her arrange meetings, and she had a feeling that without him, the native population would have been much less trusting of her.

So it was only fair she should check on him and see if he was okay, right? She'd just pop in and say hi, ask him about his day, maybe tell him about her plans for the next week. If she saw he was all right, she'd return straight back to her room and... Adriana let her forehead touch the cool black surface of the door. She'd probably return here and stare at the ceiling, unable to fall asleep while she pictured him changing his clothes, showering, sleeping next door.

Before she lost her nerve, she touched her cuff to the door panel and peered out into the corridor. It was empty; dark had fallen hours ago, and their crew was either sleeping or working, like Hanne, who was busy mapping Rendian skies.

Adriana padded across the hall; three steps was all it took, her bare feet warm on the black-tiled, heated floor. She knocked on Taron's door and then pressed the button that made a light flash inside after he didn't answer immediately.

She heard no footsteps from the other side, but the door slid sideways, revealing a bare, pale chest to her gaze. Blinking, she raised her chin to look Taron in the eyes. It felt wrong to ogle him when she'd surprised him like this.

He didn't say anything, his blue eyes dark and serious as he stared back at her.

"Hi," she said and forgot what she came here for. Then she shook her head and added, "I heard a noise. Is everything okay?"

He glanced down the corridor, then took her arm and pulled her into his room. It was the most contact they'd had for days, and as Adriana stumbled across the threshold, she tried not to grab at him, afraid she wouldn't want to let go.

The door shut behind her, and she straightened, raising her eyebrows at him. "What's going on?"

He didn't answer immediately and glared at her instead, standing very close to her, so she had to look up—*way* up. God, he was tall. And he smelled nice, that strange minty scent rising from his skin, wrapping around her senses. But she was shocked by the ferocity of his stare: Had something happened?

"You shouldn't be here."

Oh. Well, that was it, then. She retreated a step, unsure of what to do. Her back hit the door behind her. "Then why did you drag me in here?" He kept giving her mixed signals, and it was becoming increasingly hard to protect her heart from those bruises she'd feared.

"Because this needs to stop," he growled. "I'm changing the guard rotation tomorrow. I'm assigning Lieutenant Anilla to you. She's very capable. You'll be in excellent hands."

Adriana stood still. Her heart was slowly cracking in two, and she couldn't make a sound. Damn, damn, damn him. How was she supposed to react if he'd given her no explanation? She thought they were becoming friends, but she'd been mistaken.

She would not cry. Two kisses and one orgasm, although earth-shattering, did not deserve her tears. Neither did the smiles he seemed to give to her, and only her. She squared her shoulders and stared at a point several inches above his head. "May I ask why?"

There, her voice didn't tremble at all. And if he kept his gaze on her face, he wouldn't be able to see how her hands shook. She crossed her arms over her chest to keep from fidgeting.

He ran his fingers through his white-blond hair,

mussing it up. "There are things..." He broke off, glanced to the side like he was searching for better words. "I don't need distractions right now. I need to focus on—on my duties."

Adriana processed this for a moment. "And I'm a distraction?"

Taron nodded once, a curt jerk of his head, and took one step forward, cornering her by the door.

"What kind of duties?" she asked. "I-I thought I was your duty." She cringed, wishing she could take back the words. She'd sounded almost desperate, needy. And that was the last thing she wanted—even as a child, she'd learned that people didn't like it when she clung to them too much.

Closing his eyes for a moment, Taron said, "You are. You were. But there are... My brothers and I have a family matter to resolve, and I can't do that while I'm around you. I can't *think* when I'm around you."

Her breath caught in her throat. "Why?" she whispered.

He opened his bottomless blue eyes, so strange and yet so familiar. "You know why."

His voice was a tortured rasp, and Adriana touched his arm on instinct, aching to comfort him. He flinched immediately, and she dropped her hand back to her side when she saw his anguished expression.

She clenched her teeth, taking a deep breath. If he was this determined, she needed to give him space. But she had to be sure—in less than three months, she'd be leaving this planet for good, and she didn't want any regrets. And she would always wonder what could have been. There would be no do-overs of this visit.

"If you don't want me, I'll go," she said, looking him straight in the eyes. "But I would rather stay."

Standing her ground, she waited. And hoped. For what,

she didn't know. But leaving this room and returning to her own quarters would be the hardest, saddest thing.

His elegant, strong features could have been hewn from ice for all the emotion he expressed. If a battle raged inside him, he gave her no indication of it.

He didn't reply, so she swallowed a knot of hurt and nodded. "Okay." She'd find Mika and Hanne, bribe Ben to part with that bottle of bourbon he'd brought from Earth, and hole up in her room for the night. Then she'd move on with her mission and make herself proud.

Pressing her lips together, she turned toward the door.

His quiet sigh ruffled the small, wispy hairs on her neck. It was the only warning she had before his cool, strong hand clasped her elbow. "Don't go."

She faced him again, traitorous hope kindling in her chest.

"I want you so much I can't think of anything else," he growled. He raised his hand and tucked a strand of hair behind her ear, caressing it until the ends came to a stop above her breasts. He flicked a thumb across her nipple, and she sucked in a shocked breath. "Every time you get hot for me, I feel it."

Tracing his fingers lower, he slipped them beneath the hem of her pajama top, barely touching the skin on her belly. "You look at me, and I want to grab you and sink inside you so badly, I forget about everything else."

Her legs trembled, and she clutched his arms for support, the massive biceps bunching under her touch. She had no words to answer his confession, save for, "Yes."

He smiled at her, a crooked, pained grin, and put his other palm on her ass, lifting her effortlessly. Adriana clung to him, her legs going around his waist, her ankles crossed over the low spine bumps on the small of his back. Leaning in, he traced the shell of her ear with a cool tongue, sending her nerves skittering madly.

"And at night, I pleasure myself because I can only think of you across the hall."

The crude image had her gasping, and she hugged him closer, her body pulled toward his with magnetic force. Her sex pressed against his erection, the proof of his arousal so powerful it left her breathless.

"Show me."

He stilled, then groaned. He took her mouth in a fierce kiss and tortured her with his tongue, letting her know just how spectacular sex with him would be. She'd never wanted anything more.

"Show me," she repeated, and he unhooked her legs from around his waist and set her on the floor. She cried out at the loss of contact, but he was already unlacing his leather pants. Lust swelled over her, a wave so strong she trembled. She wanted to claw those clothes off him, climb him like a tree and have him take her against the wall, on the floor, anywhere, just as long as she got that long, thick cock inside her.

"Are you going to study me, Dr. Ribeiro?" he asked, lifting an eyebrow. "Make notes?"

She followed him with her gaze as he sat on the bed to take off his heavy winter boots. "I might take pictures, too."

He chuckled but grew serious again; he stood and hooked his thumbs in his waistband.

She didn't think she could hold on much longer, and he seemed to know it. With exaggerated slowness, he dragged those pants down, then kicked them off. He stood before her, naked save for his wrist cuff, the most gorgeous man she'd ever seen. Every muscle was honed to perfection by hours of training, no doubt, and his long, powerful limbs were made for battle, for survival on this harsh planet. The spiked bones of his shoulders, the savage, patrician features —he was exquisite. His skin was a faint blue, telling her he wasn't as relaxed as he wanted her to believe. At the sight of his cock, Adriana gasped.

She'd felt it, of course, had had her fingers wrapped around it, and knew even then it was impressive, but seeing it now... The length of his cock was a deep, rich blue, with a blunt, broad head that she wished to take into her mouth. Her core throbbed with a low, insistent pulse at the thought of having him buried inside her.

His large fist closed around the root, and she dragged her gaze up to his face, to his knowing smirk. He saw what the sight of him did to her; he'd said he felt her arousal, and there was no hiding from the truth. Her nipples ached, twin pebbles rubbing against the soft cotton of her top, the friction not rough enough for her. She was wet for him, her thighs slick with it, and she pressed them together in a vain attempt to bring relief.

Taron didn't say a word and sat on his bed instead. Leaning on the headboard, he gave his cock a firm stroke. Adriana stepped closer, feeling electrified, aching to touch him, but she also wanted to see what he'd do—to see what he liked. He knew best how to pleasure himself, so she wanted to observe, to learn so she could repeat it all later. She wanted to blow his mind, to imprint herself on his memory so he'd never forget her, even after she was long gone from his world.

"Come here," he murmured. He'd fallen into a rhythm now, and the rough flicks of his wrist looked almost too violent to bring pleasure.

She was powerless to resist his order, climbing onto the foot of his bed.

"Now take off your clothes," he demanded. "I've imagined it so many times already."

And somehow, that made it worse—surely he had built a fantasy version of her in his head, and her real body could never compare. But despite her reluctance, Adriana took the hem of her top and dragged it over her head. He was naked, so it was only fair.

He groaned at the sight of her, his hand moving faster. "All of it."

She shuffled out of her leggings, then knelt between his powerful thighs. Taron stilled, watching her, his cheeks flushed blue, his eyes glittering in the low light. She couldn't hold off anymore. "May I?"

He gave her a curt nod and released his cock. Her first impulse was to climb over him and slide down on his erection, but she wanted to try something first.

That changing room insanity had left her with a burning curiosity to taste him. Scooting up on the bed, Adriana took his cock in her hand, running her fingers over the smooth skin, the hard ridges below it, over the blunt head, all cool compared to her skin. Heat spread through her body—soon, she'd have him buried inside her. It was inevitable. So she ducked her head, letting her hair hide her from his view as she closed her mouth around his erection, her lips stretching to take him in.

Taron's hips bucked off the bed, and he let out a strangled groan. Then he gathered her hair to one side, and she found herself meeting his gaze while she swallowed as much of his length as she could. He was far too big for her, so she grabbed the base and set a slow, insistent pace, keeping a tight hold on him like she saw him do earlier. With her other hand, she cupped his balls, making him hiss with the pressure.

"Ah, fuck," he gasped, throwing his head back. "So warm! I had no idea—oh, shit, I didn't know it would be like this."

She grinned around his thickness and picked up her pace, reveling in the power this gave her over him. His fist in her hair, she'd never felt sexier than in this moment, tasting him, bringing him so much pleasure.

His muscles locked tight, his breaths becoming loud gasps, he muttered her name over and over again, until finally, he gripped her head and lifted his hips to her. He came down her throat, the cool liquid tasting faintly fresh, and Adriana swallowed every drop, pumping her hand, drawing out his pleasure.

He slumped back against the cushions, his big body going slack. She straightened and ran her fingers through her hair to comb it off her face. A low hum buzzed in her blood, arousal swirling, building, and she had to wonder at the chemical composition of his come. It seemed to have a light stimulating effect on her. Licking her lips, she stared down at his still-erect cock. Could she have more?

When she reached out a hand to touch him, however, Taron caught her wrist.

"You already got to play," he murmured, the only warning she had before he grabbed her by the hips and rolled over her in one smooth move, his powerful muscles bunching.

He took her mouth in a searing kiss that had her panting. Then he pulled back to trail kisses down her neck, to her breasts.

"These are even better than in my dreams." He cupped them with both hands, smoothed his thumbs over her nipples, then pressed a kiss into the valley between.

"Taron," she gasped.

He looked up at her, a wicked grin curving his lips. "I like how you say my name," he said. "It sounds foreign, somehow."

He was killing her with the chatter. Restless, she moved her hips below him, trying to get some friction over her clit, but he pinned down her hips with one hand and chuckled.

"Not yet, Earthling."

It was the first sign of what he had in mind for her. He teased her with long, cool licks that had her nipples drawing tight, and nibbled on her neck, probably leaving another love bite for her to hide. He drew her nipple into his mouth, and she nearly came from that alone—the sensation was incredible, incomprehensible, and he hadn't even touched her clit yet.

Adriana grew restless; how would she survive another orgasm with him if she felt this much already? She wasn't prepared for this, wasn't sure...

"Shh." He gentled his touch and ran his palms over her body, soothing her, yet kindling fires with his touch. "I've got you. Trust me."

Trust me. The words reverberated through her again and again as he slid down her body. *Trust me.* His breath ticked her stomach. *Trust me.* He parted her with his cold fingers, and she cried out; he leaned in and licked her clit, and she came, her orgasm overwhelming and beautiful.

She floated down to reality to find him lying next to her, watching her.

"Hi," she whispered, suddenly conscious of their nakedness.

In answer, he leaned in and kissed her temple; tears were trickling from her eyes, into her hair.

"You're salty," he said, licking his lips. "Mm. Why are

you leaking salt water?" His white eyebrows furrowed, and he took her face between his palms.

Adriana giggled. "It's called crying. We do it when we're sad."

"You're sad?" His frown deepened, a growl returning to his voice. "What did I do wrong?"

She touched his cheek, then ran the pad of her thumb over his brow. "We also cry when we're very, very happy."

His exhale was a low rumble against her naked chest. "Humans are strange."

Adriana couldn't argue with that. She supposed she was just as fascinating to him as he was to her.

Then she looked down his body to find him erect and ready, and her body pulsed in answer, satisfied but wanting more. In some aspects, their races weren't so different after all.

"You know," she said, "I've never had sex more than once in a night. I'm always so tired after. I think you're doing something to me."

He peered down at her, then shrugged. "It would only be fair."

Adriana lifted her eyebrows. "Oh? How so?"

"I'm not even sure." He flopped onto his back, his arms behind his head. "You've seen Rendian families, yes?" At her nod, he continued, "Couples are mostly monogamous, but not always a man and a woman."

"Sure, Earth couples are similar," she said, propping herself up on her elbow. She'd seen same-sex families in Volarun and also visited a woman who lived with four men. Rendians didn't seem to be very fond of casual hookups, but their choice of sexual partners was very free.

"Well, there are two..." He ran his fingers through his hair as if he was searching for the right word. "Two reasons, if I can call them that, to why couples are together. One is lust, the easiest of them."

At this, he grinned at her, and she couldn't help but grin back. Lust was definitely a major ingredient in whatever was going on between them.

"But there's also peace," he went on.

Adriana frowned at that. She'd expected him to say *love*. "What do you mean by peace?"

Taron shrugged again. "That's just it. I thought it was a sort of calm coexistence. My parents were like that—their marriage had been arranged, but they lived very happily together for years."

"Are they...?" Adriana stopped herself before blurting out the rest of that question, scolding herself for being insensitive.

"They died a long time ago. A winter sickness took them both—and nearly Lhett as well."

"I'm so sorry," she said.

Taron briefly pressed his lips together. "Thank you. But what I wanted to say was that they always spoke of their peace, of how they fit together just right. I'm not sure there was much passion between them, but now I'm wondering..."

He turned to face her, his blue eyes intense. "When I'm with you, I feel this peace, I think. It's— I feel like the world gets quiet, and I can hear myself think again. The noise turns down."

Adriana stared at him, unsure of how to react. Taron smoothed a palm over her hair, continuing onto her shoulder, her arm, her waist, seemingly lost in thought.

Frowning, she sat up. "Do you know the concept of love?" She'd never thought it would be a cultural difference —on Rendu, she'd seen parents doting on their children, friends embracing in the street. It hadn't occurred to her to question the emotions, because she'd been using humans as a reference.

A grave mistake for an extraterrestrial anthropologist. How could she assume that their society would be based on the same elemental feelings?

Taron nodded. "Yes, we love our parents and our family. Some people love their friends."

Aha, this made more sense. "So your love is more platonic than erotic."

Her comment earned her a quirk of his eyebrow. "What does 'platonic' mean?"

Adriana waved him off, not willing to go into Greek philosophy at this point. She had more important questions to ask. "So you're saying it's either lust or peace between couples."

"Yes."

"And do they ever coincide?" It would be a bleak existence living with just one or the other as a couple, she thought, especially in the long run.

But Taron shook his head. "I'm not sure, because I didn't even know that peace was a physical sensation until now. But I'd think that lust and peace excluded each other, wouldn't you say? Lust is violent and jealous, the antithesis of peace."

She didn't like where this was going. "So any relationship based on lust..." She trailed off, willing for him to continue.

"Would either mature into a peaceful union or burn itself out," he supplied, crossing his arms behind his head.

"Ah." She chewed on the inside of her cheek. She didn't want to voice her next question, but she needed to know. "So...where do you see *this* going?"

Taron's blue gaze found hers. "I don't think you'll be here long enough to truly find out, do you?"

His words hit her with full force. His voice didn't so much as tremble, and here she was, falling to pieces. It was true, he was being honest, and likely didn't even mean to be harsh, just truthful. Again, she scolded herself for assuming he would act as a human would. Adriana found her pajama top and dragged it over her head. She needed some sort of protection, or armor, for this conversation.

"I think we've found a difference in our cultures," she said, her voice small. "On Earth, we love with all our hearts."

He sat up, arms loose around his knees as he pondered this. "Interesting. What does your organ have to do with it?"

Adriana gaped. Of course, *of course*, this didn't translate well. Given what he'd just told her, their cultures were just similar enough that she'd fallen into the trap of thinking that he felt the same about her as she did about him.

Her heart thumped painfully, her hope crumbling. Maybe she should be glad of his explanation, because it would spare her a lot of grief and misinterpreted signals. She couldn't impose her own expectations on a man who felt differently than she did.

But she was falling in love with him. Every day spent together was harder to bear, and if they continued this relationship, if she slept with him, she would fall all the way—and crash, because he wouldn't be there to catch her.

She bent down and picked up her panties and leggings. She hid her face as she pulled them on, giving herself time to calm down. When she glanced at him again, she'd managed to school her features into a passably level expression.

"I'd like an early start tomorrow," she said, drawing her

shoulders back. "I want to explore some more, if you don't mind."

A flicker of confusion passed his face, quickly replaced by a neutral look. "Of course. I'll see you in the morning."

Adriana murmured, "Goodnight," and slipped from Taron's room, not bothering to check if anyone saw her leaving. It wouldn't happen again, after all. The door shut behind her, and he didn't come after her, so she curled up on her bed and refused to cry.

It would be silly to cry over a relationship that never really started. Over a man who couldn't give her what she needed—through no fault of his own. Her expectations had ruined things again, she'd put too much hope on one person and ended up disappointed, like always. She really should have known better.

But listing all the reasonable points didn't stop the tears from falling, slipping down her nose and into her pillow. She burrowed deeper under the covers to muffle the occasional sob, promised herself she'd be better in the morning, and let sleep take her into oblivion.

9

Taron

HE HAD no idea what had spooked Adriana into running away from him, but he didn't like it. He barely got any rest that night, too wired to close his eyes, so he ended up waiting for her in the mess hall, where a sleepy-eyed Hanne was eating dinner after a night of stargazing. Lhett was nowhere to be seen, so Taron supported the scientist when she swayed from exhaustion and escorted her to her room. She waved sleepily and collapsed on the bed, facedown. Taron rolled her over to see if she was breathing—who knew with humans?—and then pulled off her shoes and covered her with a blanket. Hanne didn't even move, so Taron made a mental note to mention to Lhett to take better care of his warm-blooded charge.

When he returned to the hall five minutes later, Adriana was sitting at a table with two of his crew and the blond human doctor, her laugh echoing in the otherwise empty space. Their gazes met, and she froze for a moment, then waved him over. With the table as cramped as it was, he couldn't even sit next to her and had to wonder if she'd planned it this way.

The day didn't get any better. Adriana claimed she was overdue for her weekly medical examination, which the doctor explained would include drawing her blood and having her run on a treadmill for half an hour. They disappeared into the large medical suite they'd equipped at the humans' arrival. Adriana's parting shrug left him itching to punch something. He stood in front of the makeshift medical bay and stared at the door, barely restraining himself.

He had no time for games like this. He'd told her what he felt and he'd expected agreement, if not happiness from her, but instead, she'd shut him out completely. Maybe he'd moved too soon—they'd only known each other for two months, if he counted the time spent on his spaceship. He thought they'd agreed to waste no more time, so he'd told her about the peace, which meant he was serious about her.

When he approached Kol to speak with him about this, however, his brother's expression stopped him from broaching the subject. With a jerk of his head, Kol indicated he should follow, and they slipped into Lhett's room, where they had to slap their brother awake from a deep slumber before he was conscious enough to hear the news.

"I found out what Gilmar is doing at the lakes." Kol jumped straight into the report. "He has reopened the old platinum mine at Murrun."

Taron stilled. "How do you know?"

Kol collapsed onto the only chair, rubbing his forehead. "It's better if you don't know."

This was probably true—who knew what truths the regent could draw from them by torturing Zeema.

Lhett groaned, rolled out of bed, and stumbled into the bathroom. After a minute, he reemerged, still looking only half awake, but he picked up a shirt and dragged it over his head. "I thought Gilmar was dangerous, not stupid."

"He's not stupid," Kol replied. "He just doesn't care about the consequences."

"How many people are we talking?" Taron asked.

The mines had been abandoned decades ago because the late queen, Zeema's mother, had discovered that mining would have completely destabilized the area, destroying the thermal lakes that fed and warmed several villages' worth of people. She'd decreed that no amount of platinum was worth the lives of her people, a sentiment her son carried over to his rule. Regent Gilmar clearly didn't care about that.

Kol shrugged, pensive. "It's hard to say for certain because some of the communities are nomadic, but if we only take the villages around the lakes..." He rubbed the stubble on his jaw. "Two thousand? Maybe three."

Lhett cursed. "And with half the Cabinet dead, there's no one to stop him."

"But if the general public found out? They'd riot." Taron started going through the possibilities. "We could spread the word, get them organized..."

"And risk him hurting Zeema over it?"

Taron lifted his hands impatiently. "We can't just sit back and play nannies to the humans while he destroys people's homes."

"We haven't been doing that," Kol shot back, his voice acquiring an edge. This was the voice of the heir to their family's fortune, their seat in the Cabinet. "We've been gathering information and trying to figure out how to get Zeema away from the castle without her being electrocuted." He cocked his head to the side. "What have you done, besides chaperone that pretty human around Volarun?"

Anger, heavily laced with shame, coursed through Taron's body, and he turned away, his hands on his hips to prevent himself from punching his brother. What he was implying... "I'm doing what I thought would keep Zeema alive." It was a feeble excuse, and they all knew it. He *had* become obsessed with Adriana and hadn't thought of anything else for days. All the while, his entire country was at risk of being run into the ground by a power-hungry murderer.

"So are we," Lhett said, throwing Kol a look. "It's not the right time to point fingers. If we don't stick together, we've already lost."

Taron stared at his older brothers. Lhett, the former general, was always thinking strategically. Kol relied more on his instincts, which were impeccable when it came to managing the family investments, but had landed him in trouble so often when they were kids. They were the last members of his family besides Zeema, and Taron shouldn't have lost focus. He shouldn't have become distracted, not even by Adriana.

"I'm sorry," he said, lowering his head in a gesture of deference.

Lhett's weary expression darkened as he said, "It's harder than I thought it would be." When they glanced at him, he added, "Looking after the human. Following her around."

"Yeah, you don't say." Kol rubbed his face with his hands. "She's so small. You think—how much trouble could she be?" His laugh was humorless and hollow.

Taron opened his mouth to agree, then closed it again. He couldn't really talk to them about what had happened without revealing the depth of his and Adriana's relationship, and he didn't know if she'd resent him discussing it with his brothers. He also found that he didn't want to share how much he felt for her—he didn't want them looking at her with different eyes. She was his to protect, even from them.

But a thought occurred to him. "What if we just told the humans the truth? Then they'd know why they needed to stay away from the northern settlements." Surely Adriana would understand that they were just trying to protect their queen.

Kol was already shaking his head. "I thought about it. But then Mika told me about some part of the human government... I think they're called polyp-officers? Pole-officers?" He waved an impatient hand. "Like soldiers, but anyone can call them, and they run to help. Everyone from kids onward is encouraged to report crimes."

Taron pursed his lips, already seeing where his brother was going with this. "So if they hear something's wrong..."

"They'll try to report it to the closest thing we have to that," Kol completed his thought.

Lhett's face clouded over. "Which is the Intergalactic Trade Association."

"Exactly. And Gilmar would punish Zeema over it." Kol leaned back, his head hitting the wall behind him with a dull *thunk*.

"I mean, it's not a bad idea in general, having a branch of the army organized that way," Lhett mused, probably running through the possibilities in his head. "It's worth thinking about in the future."

"Mm." Kol gave him a small, tired smile. "But promise

me you'll think of a better name for it. Polyp-officers is kind of a mouthful."

Taron snorted, leaning against the wall. "Tell me what plans you've already thought of and discarded," he said. "For rescuing Zeema."

A knock on the door interrupted their conversation. Lhett instantly looked more awake, and he stood, reaching for his spear.

"Could someone have eavesdropped?" Taron murmured, but his brother shook his head.

Kol stepped to the side, hiding behind the door, while Lhett nodded to Taron to activate the door panel.

The door slid aside, revealing Dr. Mika Yadama. Her eyebrow lifted at the sight of him.

"Is Kol here?" she asked, an edge to her tone. She peered inside before Taron or Lhett could answer, noticing Kol still crouched behind the wall, ready to attack if the intruder proved to be hostile. "Oh, so now you're hiding from me? Nice. I'm going out with the fishermen today. I'm informing you now so you won't accuse me of surprising you again."

With that, she turned on her heel and marched away, her shiny black braid swinging behind her.

Taron poked the panel, and the door slid shut. Then both he and Lhett stared at Kol, eyebrows raised, until Kol's deep-blue flush faded from his face.

"Don't even start," Kol said. Without another word, he opened the door again and stomped out into the corridor.

Taron and Lhett exchanged a glance.

"That was interesting," Taron said.

"But not surprising." Lhett yawned and stretched his arms above his head, nearly touching the ceiling. "Anything else you want to talk about, brother? I need to crash for a couple of hours before Dr. Petersen drags me out on the plains again to stare at the sky the entire night."

Taron shook his head, clapped his brother on the shoulder, and let himself out. He didn't think Lhett would appreciate a reminder to take care of Hanne at that moment.

He was no closer to figuring out what was wrong with Adriana, but his mood was marginally improved: at least he wasn't the only one who had no clue what he was doing.

It was four hours later when Adriana popped up in the empty dining hall, where Taron had been reading a report on platinum mining from two decades ago. He'd accessed the files from his tablet, hoping no one at the library would find it suspicious that he was suddenly interested in mines. He needed to be very careful while sniffing out the information. Who knew what the regent would do if he thought the Naals brothers were plotting against him.

Adriana was wearing Rendian clothes, which was enough to catch his attention, but it was her scent that invaded his mind, burrowing deep inside until his hands ached to touch her, to pull her closer so he could bury his face in her freshly washed hair and just *breathe*. That sense of peace she brought him, the calm, soothed his senses and had him relaxing his shoulders. He hadn't even realized how tense he'd been not knowing where she was.

"Did you do well in your examination?" he asked, keeping his voice quiet to avoid disturbing the others in the hall.

She nodded. "Ben says I'm completely healthy. I even broke my personal record for the distance I ran in those thirty minutes. The extra oxygen seems to help."

Ah, that explained the healthy color in her cheeks. Taron stood, suddenly unable to resist, and crushed his lips on hers. He caught her gasp in his mouth, invading her with his tongue, reveling in the warmth of her kiss. And despite her previous reluctance, Adriana responded to him, her small, warm hands gripping his shoulders. She tugged on his hair, the pain a turn-on he hadn't expected, so he picked her up and set her on the table. He ran his hands over her, tracing her curves, and drank in her every moan.

Until she broke the kiss with a shudder and a gasp, placed her palms on his chest, and pushed. She couldn't move him if she tried, but he straightened, releasing her, and stared down at her, confused.

"We can't," she whispered, straightening her shirt, and cast a fearful glance over her shoulder. "We might be seen."

That cut him deep. "You don't want to be seen with me?"

Adriana's face flushed a deeper red, her brown skin radiating warmth. "I didn't— That's not how I meant it. But we're supposed to be keeping a professional relationship, no?"

Taron stepped back and tried to get himself under control. His cock was hard and aching, but he resisted the urge to rearrange himself. He wasn't ashamed of his attraction to her—she was a stunning woman, and he was hungry for her.

But she hopped from the table, cleared her throat, and sat in the chair opposite his. "I don't want any trouble, Taron."

She wouldn't meet his gaze, so he didn't know whether she was lying to him or simply not telling the whole truth. But short of picking her up and shaking the answers out of her, he couldn't make her tell him.

He sat in his chair and regarded her in silence. Maybe she would break if he stared fiercely at her. Humans were weaker than Rendians, and he'd been told his glare was one of the reasons why his crew obeyed him without question.

But his human didn't seem to register any of this. She put her elbows on the table and leaned forward. "Listen, I've been thinking. We've been exploring Volarun for nearly two weeks now. That's one sixth of my time here, gone."

Taron's entire body froze. Was this true? She was right, of course—but suddenly, that time seemed too short. She would return to Earth, and he'd stay here; he might not even be allowed to captain the ship that would take her away from him.

She continued, oblivious to his thoughts. "I want to explore some of the rural communities. Seeing the society in a city is fantastic, but I also need to compare that to village life, you know? See how people divide work, what roles they take on, and so on." From a pocket of her wool jacket, she drew a rolled-up sheet of paper and unfolded it on the table. It was a map of the mountains, one of their own.

"I checked with Lieutenant Anilla—there are no settlements closer to Volarun than these lakeside villages right here."

Taron closed his eyes for a second, knowing where she was pointing. When he opened them again, she had her finger directly on the Murrun lakes. Where they were told specifically not to go.

His first thought was to call Anilla and chew her out for pointing Adriana in this direction, but he suspected Adriana would have found out one way or another.

"How long will it take us to get there?"

Her face was alight with the thought of new discoveries,

and he hated himself for shutting down her dreams. But it had to be done.

"It's a day's ride on a hover sled," he said, and she stared at him, eyes round, her lips forming the words 'hover sled' soundlessly. He drew in a deep breath and added, "But we won't be going there."

Adriana blinked. "Why not?"

Ah, here it was. The moment where he could tell her the truth and risk her exposing the danger to everyone, or lie and keep her safe.

"Because the villagers are very...untrusting. They're not known for receiving strangers well, especially not people from other ends of the universe."

He kept his voice level, sent a wish to his ancestors that he wouldn't turn blue at the untruth.

Eyebrows raised, Adriana asked, "Would they turn hostile at the sight of me? I haven't had any problems in the city. Everyone seemed very nice, even enthusiastic when I explained what I do."

He really should have thought this through before they had this conversation. But she'd surprised him with her plans, her questions—she was always keeping him on his toes. The innocent villagers from the Murrun area would now fall victim to his poor planning. "Yes. They're...a rougher sort of people. There aren't many of them, and with the nomadic tribes..." He trailed off at her delighted gasp.

"You have nomadic tribes? Oh, Taron, I *need* to go there!"

She was radiant with excitement, her dark eyes shining, and he felt like the worst kind of tyrant. "Are you even listening to me? They're *hostile*. You could get hurt. We get reports of skirmishes on a monthly basis. People have been known to vanish in those mountains."

Some of that light went out of her, and he wished he could bring it back.

"But... You'd be there. Surely that would be enough? Or maybe we could take more guards?"

Her tone had turned pleading, and if it was anything else, any other thing she wanted, he would have caved immediately. But now...

"I will not take you there," he said, deliberately giving his voice a rough edge. "And I won't risk my crew's lives so you can study my people like we're some test subjects."

She recoiled, her mouth opening and closing. "Is that what you think of my work?" she whispered.

Ah, shit. He hadn't meant for the words to be that harsh. "No, I—"

"Have I ever been disrespectful to anyone? Or pried into their private lives if they didn't want me to?" She got up, shooting him a poisonous glare. "I *observe*, Taron. I never intrude." She dragged her hand through her long hair, looking suddenly lost. "You know what? Forget it. I'll see you tomorrow."

Taron watched her go, aware of the stares from the handful of people who had arrived in the dining hall—their argument had not gone unnoticed. Deep self-loathing coursed through him, and he picked up his tablet and left, knowing he wasn't fit for company. Several hours of grueling training in the cold would be a fitting punishment for behaving like a total idiot.

But at least she'd be safe. He kept telling himself that through the miles he ran on the snow-crusted roads, the sharp stabs of pain radiating in his lungs. And he repeated it, over and over, when he stood in front of her door for long minutes before turning away without knocking. At least she'd be safe.

10

Adriana

"I MEAN, HOW DARE HE?"

The question was one she'd asked several times already. Mika and Hanne exchanged a look, then Hanne passed her the bowl of frozen custard, the best match to ice cream they'd managed to find on Rendu. Adriana dug in her spoon and licked the sweet, creamy dessert with a sigh.

"Okay, I'll stop feeling sorry for myself now." She'd barged in Mika's room, grabbed her friend's hand, and dragged her down the hall to Hanne's door. Then she'd proceeded to vomit up all the rage and hurt Taron had made her feel, only stopping when Hanne brought out the custard.

Now they were passing the tub back and forth—only Mika refrained because she was vegan and the frozen treat was made from rica milk. The large, lumbering animals looked a lot like yaks, and their milk was surprisingly tasty, as was the custard the cooks had provided for them.

"What I don't get is why Taron would accuse you of being insensitive," Hanne mused. "He doesn't seem like the type."

"I told him I wanted to study the rural communities around the Murrun lakes," Adriana replied. "And he told me it was too dangerous and he wouldn't risk his crew's lives so I can study his people like test subjects." Those words nearly stuck in her throat; her indignation might have faded somewhat in the last hour, but the pain had not. How had he misunderstood her work so completely? And why had he been so kind to her if he secretly thought she was doing something unethical?

Mika sat up. "Kol told me about those avalanches. So weird that people live there in spite of it, right?"

Adriana gave her a blank look. "What are you talking about?"

"I heard there are massive birds that roost in the area, so I asked Kol to take me there. He said the mountains are dangerous because of the avalanches that roll down the slopes all the time. They've been known to bury entire villages. And it's impossible to climb those peaks because you could end up setting off..." She narrowed her eyes at Adriana. "You have no idea what I'm talking about, do you?"

Adriana set down the custard. "Taron told me the villagers were hostile to strangers and I might get hurt if I tried to invade their communities. That people vanish sometimes if they go into those areas—and that the nomadic tribes attack the villages."

They both turned to Hanne, who put her hands in the air. "Don't look at me. When I talk to Lhett, he only gives me monosyllabic answers and grunts. And I have no wish to go to the mountains, thanks. I can see the stars from here."

"But it's weird that they gave us two different stories, right?" Mika said. "Why would they do that?"

Adriana remembered something else then. "When I was searching for maps of the area, Lieutenant Anilla didn't mention any of that. You'd think she would have warned me to be cautious if there was any real danger there, right? She's always been so nice to us. I can't believe she'd deliberately send me into an area that has dangerous avalanches and murderous locals."

"I'm going to murder Kol ad Naals," Mika muttered. "You'll be my alibi, okay?" She pointed a finger at Hanne, who nodded as though this was the most natural thing in the world.

Adriana cringed. "What happened?"

"He really got into the story. Told me all about how he survived being buried under an avalanche." Rubbing her face with her palm, Mika let out a loud groan. "I may have swooned a little when he said he dug himself out with his bare hands. Oh, shut up," she said as Hanne and Adriana exploded into laughter.

Hiccupping, Adriana finally sobered again. "So the fact remains that two members of our guard detail have made up elaborate excuses to keep us from going into the mountains. The question is why. Could it be a sacred site they don't let foreigners see?"

"You'd think they'd just tell us that outright and expect us to respect it," Hanne said. "I think it has to be something bad."

"Like what?"

"Mass graves from a recent genocide?" Mika offered grimly.

Adriana thought long and hard about this. "I don't think so. I've spoken to so many people these past days, and I never got the feeling they were a nation who'd do something like this. There's nothing extremist about their culture, they interact peacefully with different races from countless planets..." She shook her head. "I have no idea what it is, but it can't be that bad."

"You're such an idealist," Mika shot back. "We need to find out what's going on."

"Do we tell the others?" Hanne asked quietly. "Our delegation, I mean."

"We'd be stupid not to," Adriana said. "We'll be here for two more months. Chances are, someone is going to stumble across this secret, and they better be prepared."

So it was that they quietly dispersed the information among the human delegation. They'd decided not to hold a big meeting, which would be too suspicious, but rather sneaked minutes of hushed conversation here and there to hammer out the plan.

Their teammates reacted in very different ways to what the three of them revealed. Jean, the engineer, simply shrugged and went back to unscrewing the lid of something that resembled a large rice cooker. Steven, one of the two military specialists and their guard, seemed concerned but offered to help, while Graham, their highest-ranking member of the US Army, merely narrowed his eyes at the news. Adriana forced out a promise from him that he wouldn't alert the Rendians about this, but she didn't particularly like the guy, so she was glad when he declined to cooperate.

She kept up her previous routine of interviewing willing Rendians from various professions, and while Taron sat in on most of those conversations, he rarely contributed anything beyond the initial greetings. His manner had cooled visibly—the sizzling kiss they'd shared in the mess hall seemed no more than a dream to her now. She'd tried once more to get him to talk about the supposed conflicts between the villagers and the nomadic tribes, but he'd shut her down. This tipped her decision to go along with the plan; she might have reconsidered if he'd been willing to talk.

In the end, the idea was very simple. Adriana and Steven, the SEAL guard, would procure a hover sled and make for the nearest village, which lay seven hours north of Volarun. Since Steven had spent the past two weeks riding those very same hover sleds around the city, learning from the Rendian soldiers, the plan wasn't as crazy as it seemed at first glance.

The entire human team helped squirrel away enough supplies to last several days, including a tent and reusable heat packs. Mika even parted with a bag of vegan energy bars, her expression fierce as she shoved them into Adriana's backpack.

"You take care of yourself, Adriana Isabella Ribeiro," she said, throwing her arms around her and squeezing tight.

Adriana returned the hug. "Don't worry. We'll be back before you know it."

11

Taron

IT TOOK him nine hours to realize what she'd done.

He first came knocking on her door in the morning, ready to accompany her to her next round of interviews, but Hanne had opened the door, telling him Adriana was unwell. Retching sounds and running water from the bathroom confirmed this. When he'd tried to enter the room to see if she needed anything, Hanne placed a warm but firm hand on his chest.

"Do you really think she wants you to see her like this?" Her blonde eyebrows lifted toward her hairline, and Taron had to concede that no, Adriana probably didn't want him there at all.

It wasn't a pleasant thought.

So he'd gone to train for two hours, trying to ignore the persistent itch that seemed to crawl under his skin. He returned to her quarters and found Mika guarding the room, which was completely dark.

"She's finally asleep," she whispered. "I'll let you know the moment she wakes up, but I wouldn't hold my breath if I were you."

He didn't understand why holding his breath had anything to do with a stomach sickness—but he left, deciding he wouldn't be turned away the next time. He came knocking again in the afternoon and found Hanne on duty while Adriana threw up in the bathroom. He marched down the corridor and half dragged the lanky human doctor, Ben, to the threshold of her room.

At the panicked look Hanne sent Ben, Taron narrowed his eyes. And when Mika's voice sounded from the bathroom, asking, "Is he gone yet?" he knew they'd done something incredibly dangerous.

"Where is she?" he growled, pushing the two humans into the room and slamming the door panel to shut the door behind them. He didn't want any witnesses in case he decided to kill them all. "Where is Adriana?"

Mika poked her head through the bathroom door and went pale at the sight of him. Taron knew his skin had likely turned blue, but he was beyond caring.

"The mountains," Hanne finally whispered. "They've gone to the mountains."

Taron clenched his fists to keep from punching the wall. "Who?"

"Adriana and Steven." Ben dragged a hand through his brown hair. "We thought—"

"She left alone with a man?" Taron roared. "To the mountains? Didn't she fucking listen to what I told her?"

"She did!" Mika's voice rose, too. The small woman stood in front of him, her fists at her hips, and shouted at him, "And your story was different from Kol's. You weren't going to tell us what's really going on at Murrun, so we decided someone needed to find out."

Taron clutched at his hair. "And you decided to send Adriana? She has no military training, no experience surviving in the wild." This was catastrophic. These humans had single-handedly ruined any chance of a peaceful resolution to his nation's problem.

The regent specifically forbade them from allowing the humans to access that area. The general population in Volarun clearly had no idea what was going on at the mines, and Gilmar knew full well that the Intergalactic Trade Association would never buy platinum that came from an unethically operated mine. But Adriana would poke around, ask questions, and finally write her report, which would be made public for anyone to read. The regent couldn't permit that—and he'd already proved he didn't mind making his problems disappear.

"She was the obvious choice." Hanna's voice was quiet but steady. "She knows the people best. It would be useless to send someone like Jean, who only cares about engines. And she has Steven to guard her if—"

"Didn't you notice that Steven got assigned a guard as well? Why do you think that is?" He didn't wait for her to answer the question. "Because Rendians are superior in strength and skill when it comes to fighting. You're small and likely to freeze to death if you're left outside for too long." He cursed, adding, "And the moment something's not to your liking, you go sneaking off without bothering to ask why we were so intent on keeping you away from there."

Mika spread her arms. "Well, then, enlighten us. We were told we had the freedom to explore. Now you're telling us there are places we can't go—without giving us an explanation."

"Things have changed since your contracts were signed," he growled. He was about to explain, but he caught a glance of the sky through the window. Dusk was falling, and he was running out of time.

He straightened his shoulders and put on his commander's expression. "If you want your friends to survive, you will find Kol and Lhett immediately and inform them—*in detail*—about this plan of yours. Then you will follow their directions to the letter. Whatever you do, don't let anyone else realize that Adriana and Steven are missing."

"Are you going after them?" Hanne hugged herself, suddenly looking worried.

Good. Maybe they were finally beginning to understand what they'd caused.

"Yes. I will try to radio them and convince them to return, but at this hour, it might be more dangerous for them to turn around and get caught on the plains in the middle of the night." He turned to Ben. "What supplies will I need to heal them if they're hurt?"

To his credit, the human, whose face was now pale beneath his freckles, darted out of the room, returning minutes later with a small pack of bandages and pills. "You can call me, and I'll walk you through any procedure. I'll help you however I can."

Taron nodded and left, hearing the mad scrabble behind him as Hanne and Mika ran to find his brothers. They would know what to do—he just hoped they would manage to keep everything quiet. They needed to sweep this under the rug and pretend nothing ever happened.

Stopping in his room, he shed his clothes and pulled on his captain's uniform, activating the light armor inside it.

The surface of the suit rippled, the nano-scales forming an impenetrable protection on his body. Then he put his civilian clothing back on, piling the layers in anticipation of a long, freezing night flight across the vast lowlands that lay between Volarun and the high Dozois Mountains.

But the hardest part of this deception was putting on a pleasant smile and striding into the royal hangars where the military-grade vehicles were being kept under the eye of watchful guards. While Ben had gone to fetch the medical supplies, Mika and Hanne had explained that Steven rented a hover sled from one of the commercial posts in the lower city to avoid raising questions with the guards. This was good news, at least, as it would have definitely raised the suspicion of the regent's guards.

Now he nodded to the female soldier in the booth by the door and strode past the rows of hover sleds to where the light airships were parked at the other end of the warehouse. These aircraft weren't made for exiting the orbit, but they'd serve well for traversing the plains. If he could get his hands on one.

"Captain," one of Lhett's former trainees greeted, a man a decade older than himself.

Taron gave him a wry smile. "You know full well I'm Captain no longer, Soldier, not under the new rule."

The man exchanged a glance with his fellow guard, and they both grumbled sympathetically. Then the first one asked, "How can we help you today, then?"

Praying to his ancestors that this would work, Taron shuffled his feet and thought of Adriana to make a little color rise into his cheeks. He rubbed the back of his neck and gave the guards a sheepish grin. "It's embarrassing, really. But, uh... Can you promise to keep a secret?"

The soldiers snorted.

"Sure," the other one said.

"There's this lady in the human delegation. Small, dark-haired, curves to die for." He traced his hands through the air, hating himself for putting Adriana's image to such use, but he was desperate. "I thought I might impress her by showing her the city at night...from up above." He inclined his head toward the airships.

"Ah, I don't know about that, Cap—Mr. Naals." His brother's former soldier contemplated the vehicles. "It's an unusual request."

"But you know me, right?" Taron pressed. "And my brothers. You know I'm good for it if anything happens to it." In truth, with their assets frozen by Gilmar, Taron could barely afford to buy the steering stick, let alone the entire ship, but for once, the regent's insistence on keeping a tight lid on the entire massacre was working in his favor. As far as the general public was concerned, the Naals brothers were rolling in it.

"Couldn't you take *your* ship?" the other soldier asked.

Taron lifted his eyebrows. "The *Stargazer* takes a whole crew to run. With what I have in mind for today, I'd rather not have an audience, if you know what I'm saying."

The guards laughed, and with some more coaxing—and the promise to put in a good word with his brother—they let him have a tiny four-person ship with banged-up sides.

"I'll have it back before lunch tomorrow," he promised, though he had no idea if he'd be able to keep his word.

"She lists to the left," the guard told him, patting the gray metal nose. "And the heater's wonky, so you might have to work double time to keep your lady warm."

Taron's face muscles ached as he forced a laugh and flicked the buttons that started the ship's nuclear engine. That first hum of power was amazing; this was where he was most comfortable, this was his domain. The door to the cabin slid shut, cutting off the guards' jokes. With one last wave, Taron was off, the aircraft rising gently from its spot before he maneuvered it out of the hangar and took off into the night.

12

Adriana

"HOLY SHIT, IT'S COLD."

Steven tucked his gloved hands into his armpits, stamping his feet in the thick snow to warm himself. Adriana felt similarly frozen, the tip of her braid frosted white from their ride across the plains.

The trip had been uneventful. They'd picked up the hover sled in the city, made sure its battery was charged enough for the round trip, and set out straight toward the mountains in the distance. It was only about halfway that they realized the distance between the city and the high gray slopes was greater than it seemed—and the mountains were colossal.

On Earth, only the Himalayas could rival this sight, but these peaks rose from the lowlands with no high plateaus to soften the ascent: a sheer wall of rock that surely no living creature could climb. But tiny shapes circled in the air above the highest peaks; if they came any closer, they would probably be enormous.

"What the hell are those?" Steven asked, craning his neck to stare at the sky.

Adriana's breath puffed out in a small white cloud. "No idea," she said. "But I hope they're herbivores."

Steven shot her a look and patted the Rendian spear at his side.

They'd arrived at the village half an hour ago and waited in the village square for the inhabitants to come out. She knew Taron's warning about the hostile villagers was made-up, but she didn't want to intrude. She'd been sure curious faces would soon peek through windows and around doors, but so far, no one had come to greet them—or otherwise engage with them.

"Let's knock on a few doors," she muttered to Steven, who fell in step with her, apparently eager to move.

They went from house to house, knocking and calling, but the village was empty. That, or everyone was hiding under their beds, waiting for them to leave. Adriana swallowed a knot of unease, looking around—their footsteps were the only ones marring the fresh snow. The last snowstorm that had passed through the land had been four days ago; since then, they'd had nothing but blue skies. So it had been at least four days since anyone walked here.

"Come on," she said. "Let's try the next village."

They traveled slowly along the shore of the vast lake, the largest of nearly a dozen thermal Murrun lakes. They never froze, not even in the middle of winter, Lieutenant Anilla had told Adriana, and the villagers supplied the capital with the highly sought-after crab-like creatures that lived in their depths. Adriana supposed those were the reason for Mika's interest in the area, since her zoologist friend had been tasked with documenting the fauna of the planet.

But this evening, no boats bobbed on the steaming surface of the lake, no fishermen dragged crab traps. In fact, the eerie quiet of their surroundings gave her goosebumps that had nothing to do with subzero temperatures. Steven also pointed out that the lakeshore looked weird, as if the water had receded by several yards, leaving stone docks jutting out.

They reached the second village at nightfall, the darkness gathering around them with alarming swiftness. This village also appeared empty—there were no lights shining in the windows, and no sound came from within the darkened houses. Their sled's headlights illuminated the village square, casting strange shadows.

"This is really weird," Steven murmured in an undertone. "I don't like it. It's like they all disappeared. Like in the Roanoke Colony."

Adriana tried to laugh it off. "You've been watching too many sci-fi shows. I'm sure there's a rational explanation for all of this." She just couldn't think of one.

She grabbed a flashlight from their packs and set off to explore. "You stay here and guard the sled. I'll only be a minute." She'd dragged the man here, the least she could do was do the leg work.

Steven nodded, putting his back to the sled and crossing his arms over his chest. "Be quick. I want to get away from here and find a good place to camp."

"We could just...use one of these houses." She hated the idea of barging in without the owners' permission, but it would significantly increase their chances of not freezing their butts off.

"Yeah, okay. But we're leaving first thing in the morning and returning to the city, all right? I don't care what's happening here—it's not worth risking our lives."

Adriana nodded and set out to search for a good place to sleep. Somewhere with easy access—she didn't doubt that Steven could break in a door, but she wanted to do as little damage as possible to the property they borrowed for the night. Looking up, she thought she'd see a sky full of stars, but thin clouds obscured them this evening, heralding a change in weather. Adriana shivered and hunched her shoulders, regretting her decision to come here without Taron.

He hadn't given her a choice, though. Tomorrow, she would return to Volarun and find out what was happening here. She wouldn't take no for an answer—she would demand an explanation from Taron or the queen herself if it came to that.

She was turning back, intent on retracing her footsteps in the snow, when Steven's shout rang out. Adriana clicked off the flashlight, froze in place, and listened for any sign of danger. For a moment, she thought about calling out to him, then remembered all the horror movies, where 'Hello, who's there?' ended up being a homing beacon for the monster hunting its prey. She glanced around, searching for cover, then remembered the footprints.

Biting back a groan, she frantically tried to smudge her trail to obscure her location. What had surprised Steven, a fully trained SEAL? Was he even alive? She needed to circle around and see what was going on in the square... She looked up. Maybe she could access a rooftop and get a view from above?

Voices sounded from around the corner. Male voices, Rendian, hushed as if they were trying not to spook their prey.

Shit, shit, shit. Adriana plastered herself to the wall, only too aware of her disadvantage. While she was in good physical shape courtesy of the training for this research trip, that training mostly included running and weight training, building up her stamina, not combat training. She didn't think the tai-chi classes she took in college prepared her for fighting off six-foot-four Rendian thugs.

If she disappeared from this village, nobody would find her body. Sure, her and Steven's team members knew where they went, but the Rendians had warned them several times not to venture out into the wilds alone. *Stupid.* She thought of Taron. Would he be disappointed if she never returned? Would he come searching for her?

The voices came closer, and her heart rate spiked, her lungs seared by the frigid air she gulped down. She might never see Taron again. The thought was unbearable, and she put her mitten over her mouth to smother a gasp of pain.

It hit her then that she wasn't even worrying about not returning to Earth or seeing her parents again—no, her thoughts were all for one tall, blue-skinned alien who'd shown her so much care and attention in these past weeks. No man had ever made her feel so cherished and loved. The moment of clarity was instant—and possibly futile, if she was going to be killed here. It didn't matter what he called his feelings: peace, love, none of it was important when she *felt* his affection in every touch, every look he gave her.

But in the end, she didn't even get a chance to fight. She was backing off from the voices, trying to make a run for it, to fight to return to Taron, when she turned around the corner of the building and came face to face with a Rendian man in a soldier's uniform. He grinned at her, and before she could punch his throat, he leveled his spear at her and shot a bolt of electricity into her abdomen.

Pain seized her, locking her muscles, and she would have screamed if her teeth weren't fused together. Then everything went blissfully, mercifully black.

13

Taron

FULL NIGHT FELL while he flew toward the Dozois
Mountains. Thick clouds were gathering, the first sign of a
snowstorm blowing in from the mainland in the east. Taron
cursed and willed the beat-up airship to go faster; the metal
groaned around him as if the ship was complaining at being
abused in such a manner.

He'd disabled the tracking system the moment he left
Volarun, hoping nobody would think it too strange. Then he
tried to radio the pair of humans he was chasing, but only
kept getting static in response. This didn't bode well—either
their radio was disabled or the snowstorm currently shaking
his ship was becoming a full-blown electrical ice storm. He
didn't like either of those options. He debated putting on
the ship's headlights, but that would only alert the soldiers
at the mine of his arrival, and he didn't think anyone else
would be stupid enough to fly in the dark. No, he was the

only crazy person going into enemy territory alone and virtually blind.

It hadn't even occurred to him to stay in the city. He tried telling himself he was doing it to cover his own failure, his own inability to keep the humans from discovering what was really going on. To save his queen. But the truth was he only thought of Adriana. He needed to get to her, needed to make sure she was safe. Even though she'd left with another man without informing him. Had even deceived him to escape.

Landing the aircraft in the middle of the village square, Taron jumped into the snow. The first thing he noticed were the twin sets of footsteps. The larger set, though smaller than his, likely belonged to the soldier, Steven, and the other, small pair was undoubtedly Adriana's. He felt some small measure of relief at this—at least they'd made it this far without dying. But they weren't here anymore.

Taron glanced around, his eyes growing accustomed to the darkness. Nothing moved here. The houses stood dark, empty husks devoid of life. This raised the hairs on the back of his neck—despite the late hour, the village should have been showing some signs of activity. But no. Whatever Gilmar was doing at the mine had affected these people already.

After making certain that Adriana and her guard had indeed left the village, he climbed back on board and took off, flying as low to the ground as he dared, fearing he'd miss their next target. Had they used common sense and tried to find lodgings at the village?

At an echoing shriek from high above, dread settled in his gut. What if they'd been snatched by a mantora? The large flying monsters didn't normally attack Rendians, but they might see humans as a tasty, exposed morsel, especially now winter was slowly setting in. In that case, he would likely find their hover sled abandoned, crashed somewhere.

He pushed the airship faster, barely avoiding an outcropping of rock, until the shape of the second village materialized from the dark. Here, the prints in the snow showed a chilling story.

Adriana and Steven had clearly stopped in the square, just as they had in the previous village. Steven hadn't ventured far from the sled, if his footsteps were any indication, but Adriana's path disappeared into the dark. Much more concerning was the presence of four more sets of prints, large and wide, that Taron recognized as Rendian winter boots. Soldiers' boots. They'd churned up the snow in the square, and there was an imprint of a body that had lain in a drift. No blood—but then Rendian spears didn't need to pierce the skin to hurt or kill. He had no idea what a stunning shot would even do to a human—they were frailer than Rendians and might not even survive a full blast.

Three soldiers had followed Adriana—Taron traced her footsteps, dread gathering in his gut—and after a while, one man had split from the other two to wind down a narrow alleyway. When Adriana's footsteps veered suddenly off-path, Taron understood she must have heard her attackers and tried to hide, smudging her prints. But she wouldn't have been able to—Rendian soldiers were used to tracking in the snow.

And there it was, the spot where they'd caught up with her. Taron found the third man's footsteps on the other side of the house and swallowed back the bile that rose in his throat. She likely ran straight into him. Ah, shit, she must have been terrified. Rage boiled inside him, burning—he would find these men and make them pay for hunting her like an animal, herding her into a trap.

But he had to find her first.

An indentation in the snow showed him where she'd fallen, and a trail led from it where the men had dragged her —unconscious, he prayed, not dead.

That was his only hope going forward.

It wasn't hard to track the soldiers from then on. They'd taken the hover sled, but their footsteps coming into the village showed him exactly where to fly. And when a glimmer of light became visible through the darkness, Taron landed his ship and took off on foot, his spear out and ready.

He approached the watchtower from the side after circling it to count the guards. With the storm blowing through, there were none on the wall; instead, two of them huddled in a small gatehouse. Creeping up to the air vent, he coughed loudly, prompting one of them to come outside to check. The man was unconscious within seconds, and Taron slipped through the open door, incapacitating the second to prevent him from alerting the soldiers inside the tower.

He considered leaving the first one in the snow, but he hadn't come here to kill. Dragging him inside the hut, he took their communicator and wrist cuffs, closed the door, and fried the panel with his spear's electrical pulse, effectively locking them inside.

The guards' wrist cuffs unlocked the door of the tower— shoddy security, but then they were standing guard over an empty wasteland, likely stationed here to provide a refuge for anyone who might get caught in the weather while traveling farther north, to the mine at Ozun.

Taron crept down the corridor, listening for the guards' voices. The lower level was deserted and cold, but a light shone from the stairwell that led up. Lifting his feet carefully so his boots didn't scuff on the gray stone, he ascended the stairs, then peered around the corner.

A guard sat in the corridor in front of a closed door, his attention on whatever was happening down the hall, where the sounds of conversation were coming from. It was warmer here, and light, and Taron knew he'd have maybe a second to strike before the guard raised the alarm.

"Hey, I want a turn with her, too," the guard called.

A second later, Taron clamped a hand over his nose and mouth, cutting off his air supply. The man struggled briefly, but Taron pinched the nerves in the back of his neck, rendering him unconscious. Fools, their armor wasn't even activated. They were so secure in their superiority, they hadn't thought a Rendian might arrive to help the humans.

Taron's own armor glinted lightly at his wrists, and he wished now he'd shed the bulkier clothes he'd piled over it. Judging by the sounds of the men inside, there were at least three more in the room at the end of the hall.

He needed to find Adriana and get out of there. He didn't dare press the guard's cuff to the door panel—if it beeped, it would alert the soldiers at the wrong moment. If Adriana and Steven were locked in that room, they were better off staying safe inside it.

He neared the door at the end of the hall, trying to decide on a strategy. If he barged in, he'd have the element of surprise, but he didn't know the layout of the room. Instead, he lifted his fist and banged it on a metal panel inlaid in the stone; it made enough noise that the conversation in the room stopped.

"Keep him quiet, Keeve," a voice grumbled.

Taron banged again. *Come on, check what's going on.*

And there was the first soldier, appearing at the door. Taron slashed his spear low, catching the man below the knees, tripping him up. He went flying, his arms flailing, and crashed to the floor with a dull thud.

This was enough to get his fellows' attention. Taron stayed in the corridor to prevent them from attacking him all at once. If they did, they would only get in each other's way. Fists flew, power sparked from the soldiers' spears, and Taron narrowly avoided getting decapitated by a big brute of a man who bellowed and threw himself into the battle with the ferocity of a horeen.

Then Taron caught a glimpse of Adriana through the door. She was lying on a large table in the middle of the room, unconscious or even dead, half her clothes missing.

Taron's world narrowed down to a single thought: Kill them all. He saw the strikes against him in slow motion, rage fueling his strength, and he flicked the power of his spear up to deadly, determined to end this fast. These country soldiers were no match for him—the general himself had trained him, and Lhett was never known to be kind to his brothers in sparring sessions.

A cut here, and blue blood splashed across his gray wool jacket. A stab there, and a body crumpled to the floor, a charred hole where an eye used to be. The last soldier tried to flee, but Taron stabbed the coward from behind, severing his spine. His jaw clenched tight, Taron stepped over the bodies to the unconscious soldier slumped in his chair, and plunged his spear into his heart. He'd said he 'wanted a turn with her,' and the thought was enough to freeze the blood in Taron's veins.

Breathing hard—not from the strain of fighting but from the rage that gripped his insides—he crept forward, checking the corners of the room first for any hidden soldiers. There were none, and no other exits from the room.

Only then did he allow himself to focus on Adriana. Her small body rested on the table, her warm jacket and pullover gone, only a thin sleeveless top covering her torso. Her leather pants were obviously just being removed; her lower legs were still covered, but her panties peeked out above.

Taron checked her pulse and was reassured by the warmth of her skin, the steady rhythm of her heartbeat. She was alive.

He gathered her close, held her for what could have been minutes or hours, relief coursing through him. Burying his face in her unbound hair, he inhaled her sweet scent, letting it soothe his bloodlust.

She didn't stir. A large round welt had formed on the side of her belly button where the shock from a spear must have struck her. He didn't dare touch it; the skin was pink and tender, and he didn't want to hurt her.

He'd have to call the human doctor and ask him for instructions on how to treat this. If she were Rendian, he'd press some snow onto the blister, but with humans, who were so warm, he had no idea.

But they needed to get out of there first. Taron dressed her gently, forcing her limp arms through sleeves and tugging up her pants. Boots followed—he didn't dare take her outside without serious insulation, even for the short trek to his airship.

At last, he pulled her red beanie over her head and lifted her in his arms. Her warm weight felt good against him, and he finally allowed himself a deep breath, the first since he'd discovered she was missing.

He was walking down the corridor, weaving between dead bodies on the floor, when a groan from behind a door had him pausing. There it was again, a grunt from the room off the hall. Placing Adriana gently on the floor, he unhooked his spear from his belt and tapped the stolen handcuff on the door panel.

The room was a holding cell, currently occupied by none other than Steven, the human soldier. For a moment, Taron was tempted to leave him there, chained in the corner like some animal, but he had need of him elsewhere. Even if he'd failed to protect Adriana and had been instrumental in her escape from the capital.

Either the soldier hadn't been hit as hard as her or his larger physique allowed him faster recovery, but Steven was definitely stirring while Adriana was still unconscious. Taron cast around for the keys to the chains and found them strapped to a dead guard's belt. The blue blood that had pooled around his body was already congealing, turning viscous and dark, and Taron wiped the keys as best he could before unlocking the human. Still, his palms were blue by the time he was finished, and he wanted nothing more than to scrub himself of the filth of these soldiers.

He had to slap Steven awake, and the man twitched uncontrollably from the effects of the spear's shock.

"You'll be fine in a couple of hours," Taron assured him as he offered him a hand to get up.

Steven didn't accept it—and even glared at him, at the guards lying dead on the floor. Then his gaze snagged on Adriana, and he leaped forward, probably to check on her.

Taron grabbed him by his hood. "Don't touch her."

Steven flailed before getting his feet under him. "What the hell did you do to her?"

Rage boiled inside Taron, rage at this insignificant lump of meat whose idiocy had nearly cost Adriana her life.

"I didn't do anything. You did this—you almost got her killed. Raped." The soldier paled, but Taron rolled on. "You flew into this territory with your headlights blazing, didn't you? Did you even stop to think who might be watching? I don't know what training soldiers receive on Earth, but our children would have known better."

Steven opened his mouth and closed it again. "Dr. Ribeiro said..." He swallowed. "She said it was safe. But I shouldn't have gone in blind," he added, hanging his head.

Taron picked up Adriana and carefully settled her against his chest. He stood over Steven, watching him for a second, then jerked his chin toward the door. "Come on. I have a job for you." If the human could do this one thing right, Taron would consider forgiving him.

They descended into the courtyard, where they located the guard station's own small aircraft. Taron arranged Adriana so she sat propped up against the wall, her head nodding to the side. He tried to stamp down his worry; she'd been stunned, so it was normal for her to be unconscious. Then he pried open the engine compartment and removed a thin yellow wire from the control panel. He launched it as far as he could and watched it disappear in a snowdrift. It wouldn't ruin the ship but it would prevent anyone from using this ship to track them.

Steven stood next to him, gaping at the ship's gently pulsating nuclear core. "Is this...is it safe?" He glanced at the snowdrift and swallowed. "Are we going to get radiation poisoning?"

Taron snorted. "Of course not. We're not idiots."

"And the..." The soldier pointed back at the guard house. "The bodies?"

"We leave them here. We cannot linger. I opened the doors and windows, so if we're lucky, scavengers will come to feast and destroy some of the evidence." He'd been careful not to get cut, and for once, the brutal weather might work in their favor, wiping away any trace of Adriana and Steven. And if not... Well, he couldn't worry about that now.

Then a thought occurred to him, and he turned toward the guard house. There were two more guards locked in there, unconscious, but they'd be waking up sooner or later, and that door wasn't going to hold them back forever. They hadn't seen him when he'd attacked them, but they would raise the alarm, and soon this place would be crawling with soldiers.

"There's something more I need to do."

He strode over to the guard house and blasted through the lock with several concentrated pulses of his weapon. Then he stared at the two soldiers on the floor.

They weren't among the ones who'd been undressing Adriana, but that didn't mean they wouldn't have participated in the act. And they were witnesses he couldn't let live.

Steven touched his arm. "Let me."

Taron glanced at the human; his face had gone hard, and his lips were pressed together. But he nodded and inclined his head toward Adriana. "Go get her."

Taron turned his back on the guard house without a second thought and strode forward to get his woman. From behind, he heard first one electric *zzwap* and then another. The human soldier had done as he'd promised.

Taron hoisted Adriana back into his arms and pressed his nose against her cheek; her skin was going cold, he realized with alarm. He needed to get her to safety, and fast.

Steven joined him at the hover sled. "Will this take all three of us?" he asked.

"No."

The soldier frowned. "What?"

"I have a ship half a mile from here. I'm taking Adriana, and you're returning to the city as soon as the storm blows over." For a moment, Steven looked like he might object, but he fell silent at the glower Taron leveled at him. "You will return to the last village—you should reach it before the worst of the snow. Find shelter wherever you can, and don't freeze to death. I don't care how you do it. Then you'll race back and pretend you and Adriana never left the city. You were sick, stuck in your room the entire day."

Then he explained the bare bones of what had happened to the late king. Steven's broad, honest face paled at the story, and finally, Taron was convinced the soldier understood the gravity of the situation.

"Is that where all the villagers are?" Steven asked. "At the mines?"

"Most likely." Taron hoped it was so—and not something more sinister. "Earthlings will die if the truth about your trip is revealed. The regent can't afford for this news to get out, because the Intergalactic Trade Association would remove him immediately. Accidents would happen out in the snow, no doubt," he added to drive the point home. "Report to no one but my brothers, is that clear?"

"Yes, sir." Steven's hand twitched at his side. "Are you sure... Will she be safe?"

Taron growled at him, would have slammed him against the wall if he weren't holding Adriana's limp form. "She's mine to protect."

A muscle jumped in the soldier's jaw before he nodded. "You seem like an honorable man. But if anything happens to her, we *will* come after you. I don't care how big you are."

Taron snorted. "I'd like to see you try."

Steven watched him for a moment longer, then turned

to the hover sled. Within seconds, he was zooming off and was swallowed by the swirling snow.

Despite everything, Taron wished him luck. If his part of the plan failed, they were all doomed—search parties would be organized, and the regent would know Taron's crew didn't have enough control over the human delegation. And only ancestors knew what he would do next.

So he sent a prayer to the sky, for the human and for Adriana. Then he clutched her tight to his chest, tucking her face into the crook of his neck, and carried her into the night.

14

Adriana

SHE WOKE, and the world was upside down. A gradual awareness crept in, pain blooming in her abdomen, and cold, freezing cold, announcing where she was. *Rendu.* The swaying took her longer to decode, the crunch of snow, the fact that she was indeed hanging...she was staring at someone's back.

Adriana gasped, struggling. Instinctual fear washed over her, and she kicked and flailed, connecting with a body impossibly, unnaturally strong—until suddenly, hands gripped her around the waist and she sailed through the air, landing in a soft, cushy pile of snow.

"Oof!" Adriana wiped her face, spitting, and looked up to find Taron scowling above her. *Oh. Oh, shit.*

"I can explain." The words tumbled out of her mouth before she could stop them. Memories came back to her in flashes, the empty villages, footsteps in the snow. *Damn it,*

Ribeiro. She'd been careless, reckless. Too certain nothing bad could ever happen to her. And now...

She glanced around, panic spiking inside her again. "Where's Steven? We have to go get Steven!"

Taron's disgusted grimace was no answer at all, but he didn't say a word, only reached down to tug her to her feet. He didn't let go of her hand and nearly dragged her behind him, so she had to half skip to keep pace with his long strides.

"Taron, I'm sorry, but we have to go back. We can't just leave him there. He's a good man, he's got a mother who cares about him—"

"He already left." Taron's voice was cold, the words clipped and angry.

"What do you mean, he left?" She struggled against his grip, trying to get him to stop, but he showed no signs of slowing. "Wait, what about the soldiers? What happened?"

Ignoring all her questions, he led them behind a cluster of rocks—an airship stood in front of them, covered with two inches of snow. Taron poked a sequence of steely buttons, and the door to the cabin slid open, revealing a small cockpit with four worn cushioned seats and a cramped cargo hold behind them.

"Get in." Taron glanced away from her, his expression unbearably devoid of emotion.

When she waited for him to explain, to tell her *something*, he went to grab her waist again, no doubt to throw her inside. "Wait, stop," she gasped. "I'll go by myself."

He let her climb aboard, then strapped her into a seat with the fast, efficient movements of a man who had done this a hundred times before. Hoisting himself up, he closed the door and slid into the front seat.

Adriana leaned forward, unable to quell her curiosity. "Where are we going?"

No answer from him. Instead, he put his palms on the pad in front of him, and the ship juddered to life. The panel glowed, illuminating Taron's face with green light, making him seem even more unearthly. His strong jaw was shadowed, the planes of his cheekbones sharp and proud. She couldn't see his eyes—and her insides clenched at the realization that he hadn't looked her in the eyes even once since she'd woken up.

"I'm sorry," she murmured. "I'm sorry I left, Taron."

His shoulders tensed beneath his clothes, but he gave no other indication he'd heard her. Instead, he guided the ship up, straight into the churning night sky.

As soon as they cleared the shelter of the rocks, wind hit them at full speed. Taron's fingers twitched over the controls, but the tiny ship swayed and bucked, and Adriana was soon grateful she hadn't eaten anything since she and Steven had shared a hurried lunch of protein bars hours ago.

They fought the storm, flying low—she assumed he had some navigation system steering him, because around them, there was only darkness and snow, the wind blowing so fiercely the ice shards flew horizontally, buffeting their windshield, crusting it with layer upon layer of ice.

She didn't dare ask Taron if they'd be all right—didn't dare break his intense focus. She'd admired him when they had traversed deep space and traveled past the stars on his large vessel, but this...this was a level of skill she hadn't dreamed he possessed. If it weren't for him, she'd be dead already.

She suspected he'd saved her life earlier. No memories surfaced about the time between getting hit with that electroshock and waking up hanging over Taron's shoulder, but *something* must have happened to those soldiers. Apart from the sore blister on her stomach, which she'd covered with a nonadhesive bandage, she was uninjured. She took a couple of ibuprofen for the burn—and the headache that crept through her skull—but didn't dare complain. Who knew what he went through, what he did to bring her here?

In the dim light of the cabin, she saw the blue spots on his woolen clothes and swallowed. *Blood*.

"Are you injured?" she asked, a knot forming in her throat. She couldn't bear to see him hurt.

"No."

One word only, but it was enough for adrenaline to crash in her veins. She sagged in the seat, her hands releasing the armrests; she wasn't even aware she'd been gripping them so tightly.

She must have dozed off, because the spaceship was on the ground when she next looked through the window. The world outside was a maelstrom of snow, and though the engine had stopped, the ship trembled with every gust of the wind.

"Where are we?" Adriana fumbled with her seat belt but couldn't figure out the latch, her fingers clumsy against the cold metal. She was shaking, her breath puffing out in white clouds.

Taron unsnapped his own belt and turned to her. "We need shelter. The storm is too strong to go on tonight, and the heater's not working well." With that, he undid her buckle, his hands brushing hers. With a growl, he grasped her fingers. "Fuck, you're so cold."

Adriana yelped as he grabbed her by the waist, opened the door, and took her outside into the blizzard. He wrapped his arms around her, protecting her face from the worst of the ice, but crystal shards struck her skin, stinging, biting, and she gripped his jacket, burying her face into it.

It was rough going; Taron's legs sank thigh-deep into the snow, and by the time they reached a mound of snow, even he was panting with effort. Adriana looked around, squinting into the dark; she wished she had ski goggles for this. Everything around them dissolved into snow and mist, and she couldn't even tell where the mountains were, let alone which way the city lay. She hoped to God Taron knew where they were because she was lost, completely lost on a hostile, frozen alien planet.

She sobbed into his throat, panic suddenly rearing up, clawing at her insides. "I'm sorry," she whispered over and over again. "I'm sorry."

Taron cupped the back of her head with one large hand and pressed her closer for a moment. "We're here," he murmured into her hair. Then he gently set her on her feet and knelt in the snow.

For a wild moment, Adriana thought he meant for them to stay there, to remain forever frozen in the wild. Tears crystallized on her cheeks, stinging them, her eyelashes becoming heavier. The swirling darkness pressed down on her. She might have been one of the first humans to walk on Rendu, but she didn't want to be the first human to die here, too.

"Taron?" Her voice was carried away by the wind, and she hugged herself, trembling.

Then Taron stuck his head inside a snowdrift—no, it was a hole in the snow. He swept his hands over the small mound that attached to the bigger cupola and turned back to glance at her. "Come on."

He'd found an igloo.

Adriana dropped to her hands and knees, following him

inside. The wind died down the moment they entered the short entrance tunnel, and by the time they reached the big central chamber, the stillness of the air, the quiet, was complete. Adriana felt like her ears had been stuffed with cotton wool; after the howling wind outside, the silence rang in her ears.

It was pitch-dark, the only illumination coming from Taron's wrist cuff, but the feeble light allowed him to find the lantern standing on a shelf and light it.

A red glow lit the chamber, and Adriana stared. The round room was tall enough for Taron to stand in, just barely, and some twenty feet wide. The floor was covered in rugs and furs, the shelves hewn from ice stocked with some basic items like dried food and canteens for water. There was even something that looked like a small camping stove, likely for melting snow, and a couple of bowls.

"I need to check the vents. Stay here."

Taron disappeared back down the corridor, the leather door flaps that served to protect from the drafts swaying behind him. Adriana turned in a circle, rubbing her chilled hands together. *Wow.* A real igloo, a shelter against the raging weather outside. Were these scattered around the plains, their locations known? Or did Taron stumble across one by sheer chance?

A rasping noise near her head alerted her of Taron's work; the small ventilation hole was soon cleared of the newly accumulated snow. She wondered about the heat retention of the snow house, about oxygen levels and the force of the winds outside, her mind drawn to mundane facts of physics to calm the remaining panic inside her, the shame and guilt she felt for having drawn Taron into this mess.

She faced the entrance tunnel, awaiting his return. She would apologize again, explain...

She didn't get a chance. Taron crawled in, shaking snow off his clothes, took one look at her, and pounced.

There was no other word for the intense kiss he planted on her lips. He ravished her mouth, gripping her face with rough palms, dragging her closer, closer, until their bodies were flush with each other and she clung to him, trying to keep up.

And when he finally released her, the dark look in his eyes had her trembling—not from cold but from breathless anticipation, from awareness of him that seemed almost electrical.

"Get on the floor. Now." His voice allowed no argument, and Adriana obeyed.

Kneeling in front of him, she gazed up at this beautiful alien, this *man* who had flown in to save her, who had protected her and cared for her, and said, "Yes."

15

Taron

HE COULDN'T STOP STARING at her. Adriana knelt at his feet, her dark eyes large as she gazed at him, her lips parted and swollen from his kiss. She was the most beautiful woman he'd ever seen, and he wanted her so much his entire body thrummed at the mere sight of her. But when they touched... Her warmth burned him, scorching like a star, addictive and dangerous.

He wanted her mad with lust, so she could know what he felt every time she looked at him. He wanted her undone, screaming his name, so she would feel a fraction of what he lived with every hour of every day.

Removing his jacket, he tossed it to the floor behind her, adding another layer that would cushion her back when he fucked her. But not yet. Not until she was breathless with want.

With slow, deliberate movements, he removed piece

after piece of his clothes, never taking his gaze off her. By the time he slipped his arms from the sleeves of his uniform, she was breathing hard, every exhale still forming puffs of white in the air. He wasn't worried about that; the snow house was built to retain the heat of their bodies—hers more than his—and the red lamp he'd turned on was already warming the chamber.

And he would keep her warm. He would get her burning hot, then plunge inside her. The thought of it had him aching, throbbing, barely keeping himself together.

He removed the uniform, and she gasped at the sight of him. Her delicate features were illuminated by the red glow of the heat lamp, but he would have bet his spear and ship that her cheeks were flushed.

He was still too far away for her to touch, so he grasped his cock and gave it a slow tug, watching her for reactions. Her fingers twitched on her knees, and her eyelids lowered, her expression becoming hazy with lust.

"Taron," she whispered, his name a sigh and a plea.

But he would not give her what she wanted, not yet.

"Undress yourself." He barely recognized his own voice. Tightening his grip on his cock, he started a steady rhythm as she hurried to obey.

Clothes flew, and within seconds, Adriana was naked in front of him, the most gorgeous sight he'd ever seen. She grinned at him, but he couldn't return her smile, couldn't think beyond the pure, blazing lust.

Her body was exquisite, he'd known that, but to see it now, offered before him... Her nipples were tight buds in the cold, and goose bumps formed on her soft skin. Her hair, unbound, fell past her shoulders, brushing the tops of her breasts. He trailed his gaze down her taut belly to her generous hips, to the narrow strip of dark curls at the apex of her thighs. Her knees spread wide open, she waited for him, apparently content to let him set the pace of what was to come.

He stepped forward until his cock was level with her face; her eyes never left his as she opened her mouth and allowed him to guide himself inside. She kept gazing at him, inhaling through her nose. He gripped her hair, holding her head in place, and slowly fucked her hot mouth.

He had no words. The entirety of his being narrowed to that incredible sensation, to the pull of her lips, the low tremors of her moan coursing through him.

Pumping his hips forward, he let himself go, and when she gripped his ass, tugging him closer, he came, shouting, bracing one hand on the icy ceiling above him to keep standing. She drank down every last drop of him, drawing it from him with languid licks of her tongue.

He'd wanted to come first, to let her wait, to punish her for disobeying him, but she peered at him from beneath her lashes, a smug smile tipping the corners of her mouth up. "Mmm," she purred and touched her tongue to her lower lip.

Taron narrowed his eyes. She should have been contrite, jealous of his pleasure, but instead, she threw her head back, moaning, her hands restless on her body, one palm rising to cup her breast and the other dipping between her legs, her fingers slipping into those dark curls.

"Taron," she moaned, "You're incredible. Oh, my God, this is the best drug I've ever had."

He'd done this to her and he hadn't even touched her yet. Taron watched, his cock still hard and aching, as she circled her clit faster and faster, the movements becoming frantic, stuttering, then reached deeper to plunge her fingers inside her. She came with a strangled cry, her hips rocking, her throaty moans reverberating through the chamber.

Taron dropped to his knees in front of her, palming her head to bring her close, and kissed her, swallowing the sounds of her pleasure. And she melted against him, warm and supple, her scent driving him insane.

She gazed at him from heavy-lidded eyes as he brought her fingers to his lips and licked off the proof of her arousal, the essence of her, sweeter than anything he'd ever tasted.

He pushed her back onto the furs, the luxurious horeen pelts the perfect backdrop for her gorgeous body, and settled between her legs.

"Taron, I..." she began, but he didn't give her a chance to finish the thought.

Spreading her, he licked the slick, swollen bud, listening for her reactions.

Adriana gasped, "You're... Oh shit, you're so cold!"

He drew back, frowning. He hadn't even thought of it— was it unpleasant?

But she lifted her head and frowned at him. "Why are you stopping?"

That was a no, then. Hiding his grin against her thigh, he trailed slow, open-mouthed kisses over her skin until her thighs trembled and she tangled her fingers in his hair, tugging him to where she wanted him.

He didn't relent, even though her grip became painful— the best pain he'd ever experienced. Only when she begged him, hoarse and needy, did he obey.

"Please, Taron, please, I can't—" Her words were cut off by a moan the moment he pushed two fingers inside her, sucking her clit at the same time.

With another stroke of his fingers, another rough lick

across her bud, she shattered, his name on her lips, shuddering beneath him.

He didn't let go. Keeping his fingers inside her, he pumped slowly, brushing his fingertips over that spot that had her thighs closing around him like she couldn't decide whether she wanted to hold him close or push him away. He rose above her and kissed her, letting her taste herself on her lips.

"You're going to come until you can't come anymore. And then I'll fuck you. Again and again, so you know who you belong to. So you won't ever run from me again."

The words, rough and angry, tumbled from him, fueled by lust and rage and something far darker—jealousy and fear of losing her swirling inside him.

She stared up at him, sweat shining on her face, and opened her mouth to speak—to apologize, perhaps, or refuse him. He couldn't let her, couldn't risk her reminding him she would be leaving soon, never to return.

He kissed her again, tangling his tongue with hers, biting her lower lip hard enough so she hissed, then moaned again. He left her mouth, licking and biting his way down her throat to her beautiful breasts, drawing a taut, sweet nipple inside his mouth, sucking on it roughly until she screamed, bucking against his hand, her entire body bowing off the floor.

She grew limp in his arms, and he held her close, soothing her body and his soul. Then he brought her to another orgasm, and another. She sobbed beneath him, begging him for more, begging to let her give him the pleasure. In answer, he took her hands and held her wrists above her head, restraining her, knowing that one touch from her would send him over the edge.

"You're mine," he whispered into her ear as she crested another peak, her eyes closed in ecstasy. "Say it."

She looked at him then, her dark eyes bottomless, unfathomable pools. "I love you."

The words shattered him—they weren't what he wanted, and yet they gave him so much more.

Releasing her, he knelt between her legs, marveling at her beauty. Her hair stuck to her skin, her mouth bruised from his kisses, and yet she held her arms out to him, inviting him in.

Taron stared down at her. This was a first in so many ways, and he knew their relationship would never be the same. His life would change forever. And he couldn't back away from her even if his icy world was on fire.

With a groan, he entered her, inch by slow inch, sinking into the warmth of her body for the first time. It unmade him, the closeness, the heat, the words that he never thought he'd hear. "I love you."

With a hoarse cry, he thrust inside her, so he was fully sheathed. As he withdrew, a flush glowed all over his body. The contrast between them was incredible, his skin so dark it was nearly black in the red light, and hers brown, soft, delicate.

"I feel you," she cried, "I feel you so deep. Ah, it's— It's..."

Her words disintegrated on a groan as he moved inside her. The sensation was incredible, the squeeze of her body too intense to put into words. She urged him on, and he listened for every sigh and moan that told him how she wanted him. So he gave it to her, with increasing urgency, chasing his own pleasure.

His human liked what he was doing to her.

"More," she demanded. "Taron, you're...*oh, fuuuuck...*"

She came, her head falling back, the column of her throat exposed, and he bit her, sucked her skin until bruises bloomed on it, marks of his possession. And with her inner muscles gripping him tighter than ever, Taron lost the last shred of his control.

He snapped his hips forward, over and over, the sensation building inside him, a pressure begging to be released—until the dam broke and a surge of pleasure crashed over him, a supernova detonating inside him. Sparks danced across his vision, every nerve in his body singing, focused on her, only on her, the woman who gave him so much, who'd opened herself to him.

Breathing hard, he dropped to his elbows, keeping his weight off her, and kissed her swollen lips, slowly, gently, reveling in how she licked at his tongue. She gazed at him with sleepy eyes, drawing swirling patterns on his back with her fingertips. Her hand brushed against the spikes on his back, and his hips rocked forward on their own. His nerve endings were so fried, he felt her touch as though he was electrified.

"I love you," she whispered and closed her eyes.

Taron opened his mouth to reply, unsure of what he was about to say, but her head rocked to the side, her arms slipping from his back. He raised his eyebrows, then chuckled. She'd fallen asleep.

He withdrew from her, then covered her with the soft quilts that were stacked on a shelf, putting her socks back on just in case. He checked the ventilation shaft again and slipped beneath the blankets behind her. She didn't even stir as he drew her body close, wrapped an arm around her waist, and buried his face in her hair.

With a sigh, he settled in for a long wait—the storm

would rage all night, and they would need to race toward the capital in the morning.

But the slow, steady rhythm of her breaths calmed him. He never wanted to fall asleep without her again. Letting her go seemed impossible—but he knew in that moment that he cared for her too much to keep her if she wanted to leave.

16

Adriana

THE DIM LIGHT inside the snow house was a shade or two brighter than before, so Adriana assumed it was morning. They were still alive, not frozen to death, which was good. She was warm, even though Taron's body was cool against her back, but the thick, soft pelts and blankets had kept her insulated from the worst of the chill.

She had a vague memory of Taron getting up in the night, making sure they didn't suffocate, but she'd been too exhausted to even raise her head, let alone help him. She'd lain half awake until he was back at her side, nestled behind her, before she drifted off to sleep again.

Now she shifted under the covers, slowly turning toward him and trying not to disturb his slumber. His pale face was relaxed in sleep, his short, white-blond eyelashes twin crescents on his cheeks. The strong, aristocratic features were softened by the dim light, and Adriana ached at the sight of him.

She'd told him she loved him, and he'd said nothing in return.

A sigh escaped her lips, and Taron stirred, opening his eyes, the initial confusion quickly replaced by sharp focus when he realized he was looking straight at her.

Adriana smiled tentatively, unsure of how he wanted to proceed. As for herself, she wanted nothing more than to stay here and never return to Volarun, to the secrets and hiding their attraction. She licked her lips, probing the tiny bruise his kisses had left there the night before. With that small touch, memories rushed in, as if her body still bore the impression of his, both on her skin and deep inside.

Taron never looked away from her, and whatever he saw in her eyes must have tipped him off to her arousal, because he groaned, touching his forehead to hers. "You have killed me."

His morning-rough voice rumbled through her, and she shook her head, unable to force the words past the knot in her throat. He'd ruined *her*, bringing her such unearthly pleasure she'd nearly passed out.

She had no idea what to do. Pouring her heart out to him had been a mistake—but one she would have repeated if she got a chance to relive the night. She was leaving in two months. There was no time to waste, and she'd forever regret not telling him if she left the planet before she made her confession.

In the light of the morning, however, she didn't dare repeat those words. So she closed her eyes and kissed him, touching her lips to his, and slid her palm up his arm, over his firm biceps, to his spiky shoulder. She clung to him when he returned the kiss, his stubble pricking her chin.

With a quick move, Taron pulled her on top of him. Adriana took him inside, his long, cool erection stretching her until she could take no more. With slow rolls of her hips, she set a steady pace, her gaze never leaving his. Taron's eyes glittered in the dim light, his features taut with tension, his skin turning dark blue, the same as it had the night before—beautiful, he was devastatingly beautiful, and he had her heart.

She grasped his shoulders for support, moving faster. He lifted his palms to her breasts and pinched her tender nipples between his fingertips, and she gasped, the first sparks of pleasure already dancing in her veins. Leaning down, she kissed him with all she had, with every ounce of her being, telling him with kisses what she was too afraid to repeat with words.

But Taron seemed to understand. His big palms on her hips, he helped her move above him, surging into her from below, driving her closer and closer to that sensual cliff. And when she came with his name on her lips, her core tight around his thick, cold cock, she clung to him until he, too, tensed beneath her and came, growling.

With a satisfied purr, she lifted herself off him and toppled onto the furs by his side. Huffing, she pushed her hair off her face and smiled at him, expecting a goofy grin in return. Instead, Taron's face seemed hewn from stone, his jaw clenched as he stared at the ceiling of the snow shelter.

"Hey," she said, "what are you thinking about?"

But Taron didn't even spare her a glance. "Get dressed. We need to go."

Adriana was suddenly conscious of the cold, and she pulled on her clothes with trembling hands. What had caused this change in him? He'd seemed playful when he first woke up, but it was as if the sex had stirred up some deep resolve within him. He was dressed in a matter of seconds, and before Adriana could so much as touch him, he was stepping into his boots and heading for the tunnel that led outside.

Her insides hurt, his rejection stinging worse than she could have imagined. It was her own damn fault, though. She'd clung to him, told him things she should have kept to herself, and scared him off. Time after time, she repeated her mistakes—she thought she'd learned her lesson with humans, but no, she'd driven away the one alien she cared for as well.

Scuffling noises alerted her to his return, and she faced away from the entrance to compose herself. A moment later, he shoved a protein bar at her.

"Eat this." His voice was quiet, but the command was unmistakable.

Adriana bristled at his tone. "I'm not hungry."

"You were nearly hypothermic last night, so you need the calories. Eat it."

She opened her mouth to contradict him again, but he was already tidying up, switching off the heat lamp, and folding the blankets. Adriana unwrapped the protein bar and bit in—she wasn't stubborn enough to starve just to spite him—but the bar tasted like sawdust.

Forcing down the mealy mouthful, she asked, "How did you find this place?"

He didn't reply. She only wanted things to go back to normal, to what they'd been before she foolishly revealed too much of herself. Their 'normal' had been her asking question after question, and him answering as best he could.

But now it seemed he wasn't in the mood to oblige.

"Are there many shelters like this one? I imagine it would be deadly to get caught on the plains in such a snowstorm. By the way, is it still snowing outside?" She babbled, filling the silence because she just couldn't bear it.

Replacing the last blanket on the neat pile, he half turned toward her, and she could have sworn the corner of his mouth tipped up. It wasn't a smile, but his expression softened just enough for some tension inside her to release.

He might not feel for her what she did for him, but at least he wasn't stone-cold anymore.

"There are shelters all over the plains, but you have to know where they are to find them. In a storm, they're indistinguishable from the landscape." He motioned for her to crawl into the tunnel in front of him, and she obeyed, getting on her hands and knees, shuffling forward until she poked her head out into the clear morning.

"And no, it's no longer snowing."

Adriana barely heard him. Opening before her was a beautiful, majestic view: the impossibly vast plains of Rendu, extending to the horizon, an unmarred expanse of white. Only the mountains in the distance broke the monotony of the landscape. But for the moon, a pale violet crescent that hung high in the sky, Adriana could have imagined she was somewhere in Antarctica, standing on a mile-thick layer of ice.

Taron stood next to her, but it wasn't until she drew a shuddering breath and tore her gaze away from the view that she noticed he was actually watching her. As if she was interesting, arresting, beautiful.

"What's going on?" she whispered, no longer able to keep her thoughts to herself. "I know I messed up, and I'm sorry, but you haven't said a word to me since—"

"I said plenty last night," he cut in, his eyes darkening.

She smacked his shoulder and got a grin in return. Well, at least he was thawing.

"It's complicated." He sighed, rubbing his hand over his face. "Come on, I'll tell you everything on the way."

And he did. They cleared the snow off their ship, scraping the ice off the door panel and windshield, and Taron started talking. He told her about the late king, his cousin, and the regent's coup, about the queen's collar and his brothers' attempts to find some solution that wouldn't involve a massacre.

They climbed into the cold cabin and took off, and Taron flew higher, showing her the view from above. The black city of Volarun glittered in the distance, the spires of its palace like claws breaking through the white crust of ice, drawing ever closer. Rendians were a peaceful nation, but their capital testified to the underlying danger that they presented to anyone who would dare attack their planet. She longed to learn more about the people, their history and their culture, but this situation with the regent took precedence.

"What's your plan now?" she asked. "What will you do?"

Taron's shoulders were tense, and he kept his gaze straight ahead. "We don't know yet. First, we'll need to see how much damage your trip caused us. We were supposed to keep you on a tight leash." He snorted softly.

Adriana flushed; she deserved the censure, but that didn't mean it was any easier to bear. "I'm really sorry," she said. "I never would have gone if I'd known..."

Taron sighed, his breath momentarily fogging the glass pane in front of him. "We should have told you sooner. All of you. And I, especially, never should have kept it a secret from you for so long. I should have trusted you." He cast her a look over his shoulder. "Forgive me."

She swallowed, nodding, and put her hand on his shoulder. Keeping one palm on the ship's controls, he took her hand in his and brought it to his lips for a kiss. Adriana's heart melted, and for the first time since she'd started on this fateful trip, hope filled her. Maybe they could figure out how to help the queen and the mine workers from the abandoned villages. Maybe Taron cared for her as much as she cared for him.

She permitted herself a happy sigh—but then she noticed that while they'd been traveling in the general direction of the city, they were now making for a cluster of low structures a mile from the city walls.

Taron was taking her to the sky port.

17

Taron

"WHAT'S GOING ON?"

Taron closed his eyes for a moment at Adriana's question. She tugged her hand free from his grip; he'd kept touching her because all he could think was: *This might be the last time I hold her hand.*

Wordlessly, he brought the ship to a soft landing near the hangar—not close enough for the sentries to register a ship with its navigation system shut off but not too far to trek to the terminal.

Then he turned to face the woman who'd brought him to his knees.

"Taron, why aren't we going back to the city?" Her dark eyebrows were drawn down, lips pursed.

"I'm going back," he said slowly.

"But I'm not?" Her voice rose in pitch, echoing in the tiny cabin. "Is that what you're saying?"

He forced himself to nod even as his chest felt like it was caving open, his ribs clawed apart by a beastly pain. "You're escaping this planet before the regent realizes you've seen what he's doing at the mines." Swallowing, he kept his gaze on her chin, too raw to look her in the eyes. "It's the only way I can be sure you'll be safe. A ship will take you to Nikku. It's a short flight, and the planet is a respected merchant hub. You'll be able to find transportation to Earth with the money I'll give you."

His last savings, put to good use. She'd return home to her blue planet, to her family, where she would be warm and out of harm's way. He regretted now that he'd never asked her about her parents, about her siblings—he didn't even know if she had any. They'd always talked about his planet, his people, and there was so much he wanted to know.

But it wasn't meant to be. She would never be safe here. Not until the regent was dead—and by then, Taron would probably be dead as well, given how slim their chances of victory were.

Her sob sent a lance of pain right through him. He caught her gaze, lifted his palm to her cheek, and wiped the tears off her soft skin.

"Shh," he murmured. "Don't cry, little Earthling. I'm not worth crying over."

She smacked his hand away, her eyes suddenly blazing with fire. "Like hell," she snapped. "That's not true. Don't you ever say anything like that again."

Taron blinked in surprise. He opened his mouth to say something—anything—to calm her, but she was still yelling at him.

"I'm not going anywhere. If you think for a moment that

I'll leave my friends here to be murdered by some psychopath, you don't know me at all."

In hindsight, he really should have anticipated this. She wasn't the type of woman to accept an order of that magnitude without protest. "Adriana, I'm just looking out—"

"I don't care," she interrupted, swiping her palms over her cheeks and sniffling angrily. "I'm not going home. I'm staying here."

He scoffed. "What, forever?"

He'd meant it as a joke, as a reminder that this wasn't her fight to begin with because she'd be returning to Earth in two short months.

But Adriana sat back, crossed her arms over her chest—as much as she could with all the layers of clothes—and said, "Yes."

Hope was the worst; seductive and painful. Did she really mean it? Would she stay with him, here? He had nothing to offer her, nothing to give beyond his miserable protection, not until they deposed Gilmar as regent.

"Provided we travel to Earth once in a while," she added. "I want to spend Christmas on a beach somewhere."

Taron didn't know what Christmas was or why she'd want to stay near the sea while it was happening, but this was hardly the most important issue now.

"Adriana, you could get killed. If Steven didn't succeed in returning the hover sled..." He shook his head. "I can't risk it."

"But you would risk the lives of everyone else on the human delegation? Of your brothers?"

There was no way he could answer that. His gut churned with the thought of what would happen if he returned without Adriana—the search for her would uncover not only the regent's deception but also Taron's massacre of the guards at the First Murrun Station. It might even cause the queen's demise.

"That's what I thought."

Adriana's smug pout had him tilting forward and kissing her. It wasn't a conscious thought but an imperative he was powerless to resist. She leaned into the kiss, touching her warm palm to his cheek before she broke the contact and rested her forehead against his.

"I'm going to be okay. Now take me back to the city."

It didn't feel right, putting her in danger, but short of tying her up and tossing her onto a departing spaceship like a sack, he was out of options. If he left her here, he had a strong feeling she would follow him back on foot, stubborn as she was. And possibly freeze in the process.

"If I feel even a touch of danger, I'm getting you out of there, with or without your cooperation." He put on his fiercest frown, one that had his crew members falling in line without another word uttered.

But his human just smiled, her gaze going soft. "All right."

Damn it. He hadn't expected her to capitulate that easily. He chewed the inside of his cheek, trying to think of a way to tell her what needed to be said.

"I...I have nothing to offer you, Adriana. You shouldn't..." He released her, gripping the back of his head with both hands. "You can't make the decision if you don't know all the facts. I have nothing. Unless the regent is removed, I have no money, no home to give you beyond our rooms at the palace." The truth burned inside him, his shame rising like bile in his throat. "And even if we succeed... I'm just a captain of a spaceship. My brother has taken over the family mansion and fortune, like our parents wanted. I don't have a real home here."

He couldn't bear to look her in the eyes. Staring out the ice-crusted windshield, he clenched his fists in his lap to keep from fidgeting, from opening the door and escaping her frank assessment. She would find him lacking and return to her planet. Or worse, she would find another Rendian who fulfilled her needs better than him. At the thought, he ground his teeth. Would he meet her at the palace, see her holding someone else's hand? Would he see her with his children—*oh, fuck,* children!

He looked down at her stomach, which was obviously unchanged and hidden beneath her winter gear, and experienced the strangest sensation. Something clicked into place inside him, settling all the doubt, all the worry.

She could be carrying his child.

There was no proof their species were even compatible, no precedent to believe that such a thing was possible.

But he didn't care. Grabbing her by the waist, he hauled her into his lap, wrapped his arms around her, and buried his face in her soft hair.

Adriana chuckled, shaking against him. "Want to tell me what happened there?"

He couldn't speak, so he shook his head in wonder and kissed her again. And when she melted, grasping his shoulders and shifting in his lap to straddle him, he knew they'd be all right.

In the end, she broke the kiss and paused, holding his face in her hands. She was so close he could count the little brown freckles on her nose and cheeks. Her lips were slightly chapped, and her stare was very serious.

"Listen to me, Taron ad Naals." She spoke slowly, her voice even and calm. "I don't care if you have nothing. I don't care if we have to live on your spaceship. I don't care if we have to live on *this* ship."

She grinned at that, and Taron couldn't help but grin back.

"I hope it won't come to that."

"I'm trying to tell you that I'm all in," she murmured.

For a moment, he couldn't speak. He still heard the words she'd uttered last night in the grip of passion, and while he knew she'd meant them then, he wasn't sure if they were true in the light of day.

"Come on," she said before he could voice his thoughts. "I'm freezing. Take me back to the city."

They would have to talk, really talk about their future, but now was not the time. Taron deposited her back in her seat with a rueful sigh, making sure she was buckled in safely, then placed his palm on the control panel.

And flew them back into danger.

18

Adriana

THEY LANDED in a large hangar where dozens of small aircraft stood in neat rows. She had to wonder at the sheer size of the Rendian army if this was just one of its warehouses. How many soldiers did the regent command? What were they going up against?

The threat they were facing suddenly seemed more real.

Taron groaned at the sight of two Rendian soldiers approaching. "I'm really sorry about this," he muttered as he handed her down through the door.

Adriana only had time to send him a questioning look before the soldiers were on them.

"Welcome back, sir," the older one said. "Did you have a nice trip?"

The younger man sniggered and checked Adriana over. For the first time since landing on Rendu, she had to fight the urge to cover herself—even though she was wearing four layers of clothing.

Taron drew her to his side, his arm around her shoulders. "Yes, thank you. It was very pleasant."

"I would imagine so!" The guards guffawed, and the first one slapped Taron on the back.

"She's pretty," the younger soldier added, stepping closer.

He lifted an arm to touch her hair, and Adriana recoiled away from him.

Taron moved so fast her eyes couldn't track his movement. One moment, the guard was inches away from her, and the next, he was slammed against the hull of the ship, Taron's elbow at his throat.

"You don't touch her," Taron growled through clenched teeth.

The young soldier's eyes bulged, his face turning a mottled blue. "Stop, you're—"

"Do. You. Understand?" Without so much as breathing hard, Taron hoisted the soldier higher, until his feet no longer touched the ground.

"Sir, he didn't mean..." The older guard tried to intervene, but a furious glare from Taron stopped him in his tracks.

"Yes," the soldier gasped. "Yes, sir!"

Taron stepped back, and the young man crumpled to the floor. Adriana stood rooted to the spot, her hand over her mouth, too stunned to speak. Taron grabbed her other hand and dragged her toward the exit, not even glancing back to where the soldier was coughing on the floor.

"Taron," she yelped, failing to match his long strides. "Taron, stop."

They were outside now, the brutal chill settling around

them. The icy ground was slippery, and Adriana feared she would twist her ankle if they didn't slow down.

He halted abruptly, hauling her to him, and crashed his lips over hers.

"Mmh," she mumbled, holding on for dear life as he plundered her mouth, warming her insides with such effortless ease. She kissed him back, soothing, licking, until his rough breaths slowed and his grip on her hips relaxed from bruising to gentle.

"I couldn't let him touch you." His voice was still low, gravelly, rumbling through her like an avalanche. "No other man..." He stopped himself, closing his eyes.

She should have been appalled at his behavior. She would have dealt with that soldier on her own if he had persisted. But his protectiveness told her something he likely wasn't aware of yet. He certainly wasn't acting like he was at peace now.

"Thank you for helping me," she said, smoothing her hands over his shoulders, up his neck, until she touched his skin.

He shivered; her hands were probably freezing cold even against his skin.

There was more he wanted to say, she was sure of it, but they were standing in a public square, with soldiers milling about and civilians casting curious gazes their way. And even though the white sun was rising over the rooftops, the day wasn't getting any warmer.

So she took his hand and tugged him toward the palace, letting that kernel of truth heat her from the inside. She'd meant what she'd said earlier—she didn't care one bit about his money, and she was prepared to live the rest of her life knowing she loved him, truly loved him, while his feelings for her were a lot less violent.

Now, she couldn't help but hope. Maybe, just maybe, she could find out whether he loved her, too.

They walked into the palace through the main gate, pretending nothing was amiss: just a couple holding hands on a beautiful winter morning. Hurrying into the human delegation's quarters, they were greeted by quiet, relieved exclamations and hugs. Lots of hugs.

They couldn't risk a big meeting without alerting the palace guards that something was going on, so Taron grabbed his brothers and assured the others they would get all the information soon.

Mika and Hanne slipped into Taron's room behind them, and Hanne stuck out her tongue at Lhett when he tried to get her to leave. Adriana lifted her eyebrows at this; Hanne was the most serious of their group. If Lhett's thunderous expression was any indication, there was some serious chemistry between them.

Mika saw her looking and winked—and Adriana was swamped with guilt, realizing she'd been so absorbed in her own problems, her relationship with Taron, that she hadn't paid much attention to her friends.

Sidling closer to Hanne, she took her friend's hand and squeezed. "I'm so happy to be back," she whispered.

Hanne, taller by nearly a head, pulled her into a hug, her fragrance comforting and familiar. Mika joined the group hug, her slight body colliding with theirs, nearly toppling them over. Adriana laughed—this was her family, blood or no blood. These two would never care if she clung too hard.

"Enough with the hugging already." At Lhett's growl, they disentangled themselves and faced the three brothers.

Adriana had to admit the sight was impressive. The Naals brothers stood tall and proud, wearing similar expressions of exasperation, though Taron quirked his lips as he met her gaze.

"Sorry," Adriana said. "I'm just glad to be here."

"You should be glad you're still alive," Kol remarked mildly.

That sobered her. "I know. And I'm sorry for causing you trouble."

"It wasn't all her fault," Mika piped up from beside her. "We agreed that someone needed to investigate."

Kol didn't seem impressed. "Well, we've managed to keep the news of your disappearance contained because the regent is busy with an envoy of foreign dignitaries that arrived yesterday. You can all return to your work and pray nobody notices anything amiss."

"Um." Adriana glanced at Taron, then back at his brother. "Didn't Steven tell you...?"

Lhett tensed at this. "Tell us what?"

"About the guards?"

Kol closed his eyes for a brief moment, then looked at his youngest brother. "What is she talking about, Taron?"

Hanne put her hand on Taron's arm, earning herself another glare from Lhett. "Steven only managed to tell us Adriana was with you and safe before he was called in for a flight training with the royal guard. He had to leave; it would have raised suspicion if he hadn't."

Ah. That explained it.

Taron groaned, then faced his brothers, his shoulders straight and arms rigid at his sides, a soldier reporting to his superior officers. "The rescue of Adriana required me and Steven to kill six guards at the First Murrun Station."

Kol's jaw dropped. Lhett turned away and cursed so violently, Adriana flinched. She'd caused this with her damned curiosity. The human delegation was responsible for the death of six Rendians, horrible as they might have been, and if word got out, they would all be in big trouble.

Kol looked like he was about to start yelling, but Taron stepped forward and cut in.

"They would have raped her, Kol." He swallowed, his throat bobbing. His skin turned a dark, dangerous blue. "They were...she was half naked when I got there."

Hanne and Mika exclaimed and hugged Adriana again. She'd known there was something he wasn't telling her, but with their night and morning so fraught, she hadn't stopped long enough to ask him for the details. A tremor coursed through her, her chin wobbling, and she bit her lip to keep the tears from overflowing.

He'd saved her. Had she even thanked him for it? Their gazes met across the small room, and for a moment, everyone faded, the connection between them undeniable. This man had risked his life and flew through an ice storm to protect her.

She would never let him go.

Reality rushed in again when Hanne released her and went to hug Taron. "Thank you," she mumbled into his clothes. "Thank you for saving her."

Lhett's frown was dark as midnight. A vein pulsed in his temple, and Adriana thought he might explode if Hanne didn't stop touching his brother.

Tugging at her friend's sweater, she said, "I'm okay. But we could be in serious trouble if word gets out that Steven and I were there last night."

"Or that the flight I took wasn't just a pleasure cruise," Taron added.

Yeah. She didn't think the soldiers at the hangar would keep quiet if anyone came asking questions about Taron. He'd ruined his chances of that the moment he grabbed the young soldier.

"You've effectively forced our hand," Kol was saying. "We have to act now."

"You mean save the queen?" Hanne asked.

Mika hummed the first notes of *God Save the Queen*, and Adriana poked her in the ribs to stop. It was hardly a time for jokes, but she returned Mika's mischievous smile. It was good to be back.

"Save the queen, get rid of Gilmar," Lhett answered. "But we still have no idea how to work around that fucking collar."

"Has anyone asked Jean?" Adriana suggested. Their engineer was probably smarter than the rest of the delegation put together—and none of them were exactly average in that regard.

"You mean the silent one?" Kol seemed doubtful. "He hasn't spoken three words since he came here."

Adriana smirked. "Just wait and see."

Hanne went in search of Jean, returning minutes later with the engineer and his Rendian guard, Lieutenant Anilla.

Jean Proulx, the six-foot-two French Canadian with the body of a professional hockey player, refused to meet anyone's gaze. He wasn't comfortable around people, but it wasn't people they needed him to fix. He worked wonders with machines.

Hearing what they needed him to do, he stared at a wall above their heads, his jaw muscles jumping. But Adriana recognized the interested gleam in his eyes. This was a puzzle he couldn't resist.

"I'll need another collar like that," he rumbled, his French translated through their little ear devices.

Taron nodded, hope shining in his face for the first time. "That can be arranged."

Jean pursed his lips. "And a person willing to wear it."

His declaration was met with shocked silence. Surely he didn't mean...

"The person will get electrocuted. A lot. We will keep it set to a minimum charge, but it's unavoidable." Jean's words were devoid of emotions, a simple statement of fact. "Does the device also have a location tracker?"

Lhett nodded mutely, his face pale, and stepped forward. "I'll—"

But Lieutenant Anilla rolled her eyes, cutting him off. "Don't worry, General, I volunteer. Come on, human, let's do this." She nudged Jean with her shoulder as she turned toward the door.

To Adriana's surprise, Jean looked her straight in the eyes and asked, "Are you sure?"

The lieutenant smiled, her cheeks flushing a light blue. "No. So we need to start before I change my mind."

They left, leaving stunned silence in their wake.

Then Taron said, "Well, that's taken care of. Now we need an actual plan."

<hr />

They remained in Taron's room, taking care to walk the corridors from time to time so nobody got suspicious of their absence. They claimed they were all resting up for the banquet the regent was preparing that evening—he had invited the entire human delegation to dinner at the great reception hall in the palace—and most of the Rendian guards were happy to have the afternoon off.

Hanne brought them food, a milky stew with fat, tender dumplings swimming on top, and Adriana slurped it up without even asking what it was made of. Since she decided to remain on Rendu, she would need to get over her culinary hang-ups.

She hadn't mentioned that to her friends yet—this wasn't the right time. But she would have to talk to them soon. Ask them to deliver a letter to her parents, to explain why she wasn't returning to Earth.

Steven arrived during an intense discussion of their escape plan, and wrapped Adriana in a tight hug. She returned it until the soldier suddenly disappeared from her grip—Taron had grabbed him and flung him across the room where he landed in a heap, dazed but unharmed.

"Don't push it, human," Taron growled, pointing at Steven.

The SEAL nodded, eyes wide. "Not a problem. Message received."

But he wasn't happy with their plan, especially not the part during which Adriana and the queen herself would have to incapacitate the queen's guards.

"We'll stun them," Adriana said. "Zeema can disarm one, and I can do the other. It'll totally work. And all the Naals brothers need to remain elsewhere, surrounded by witnesses, so they won't be implicated."

The regent hadn't invited Taron or his brothers to the dinner, a deliberate slight since the foreign emissaries would be present as well. Adriana and the rest of their research team would prepare an ambush in the bathrooms adjacent to the great hall, where Zeema would only be followed by two guards, not the entire contingent that seemed to trail her everywhere else.

Then Ben spoke up from where he was sitting on Taron's chair. "You could sedate them."

Lhett scoffed. "There aren't very many substances capable of knocking out an adult Rendian, Doctor, and they're tightly regulated. I doubt our trying to procure some for tonight would go unnoticed."

Ben chewed his lip, his pale cheeks going pink. "Well..."

Adriana raised her eyebrows at him, but he wouldn't meet her gaze.

"Spit it out already." Kol sighed. "We don't have all day."

"I've been studying Rendian blood," the Dutch scientist blurted out. "I stole a couple of pouches from the hospital I visited last week, and I think I know what would work as a sedative."

In the short time she'd been in contact with Rendians, Adriana had never seen one turn a shade of blue so dark as Lhett turned now. He was on Ben in a second, pinning him to the floor, his massive fist poised to strike him. Adriana didn't doubt one hit from him would kill Ben.

"No," Hanne screamed, throwing herself at Lhett, full-body tackling him from the side.

Lhett reacted a moment before she collided with him, catching her and tumbling back, rolling to take the weight of her. Then he put her on the floor and rose above her, still enraged.

"Lhett, stop," she begged, her palms on his chest. "Let him explain."

The general heaved a deep breath, his color slowly fading. "You defended him? I could have hurt you, and you chose to defend him?" His voice was hollow, seemingly devoid of emotion, but a cold fire burned in his blue eyes.

Adriana watched him, holding on to Taron's hand; she'd grabbed it without thought, seeking comfort. He placed a palm between her shoulder blades and brushed her back to soothe her.

Danger still lingered in the room; Lhett stood abruptly and stalked into the bathroom, and Hanne, incredibly, followed him there. The low murmur of their conversation filtered through the door while everyone else waited, silent and shocked. Ben picked himself up from the floor, wincing as he rubbed the back of his head.

Finally, the bathroom door opened, and Hanne and Lhett emerged. The general fixed Ben with a murderous glare. "Explain yourself."

The doctor's face was still pink, whether with exertion or shame, it was hard to tell. "I'm sorry. But I asked a number of Rendians for blood samples, and you've all refused."

"Did it occur to you that we don't want to be studied?" Kol enquired mildly, though his lips curled with distaste.

Ben hung his head. "Yeah. And I know I fucked up by stealing the blood. I'm sorry, and I'll return the two pouches that I haven't used yet. I stored them like in the hospital, so they should be completely intact." He plopped onto the edge of the bed, his leg jiggling restlessly. "But I think you'll want to know what I found."

He looked from Adriana to Taron, his eyes shining with the light of discovery. "I'm pretty sure Rendians don't produce their own adrenaline. Their fight or flight reflex is fueled by a completely different chemical. I don't know how it's produced because I haven't had the chance to study their glands—" He cut himself off and cleared his throat.

"Er, not that I'm planning on doing that. Anyway. Adrenaline might work as either a sedative for them, or it might overload their nervous system and send them into a shock of sorts."

"So you don't *know* this for sure?" Taron asked. "This is just a theory?"

Ben shrugged. "Yeah, but it's an educated guess. I'd need someone..."

"To test it on?" Lhett interrupted, glowering at him. "Not happening."

Adriana stared at her colleague, scrunching up her nose. "Ben, that was really uncool. But do you really think it could work?"

"I'm sorry. Really. But you understand how it is, right? We're only here for another two months, and then I'll have to return to Earth and..." Ben shook his head. "I'm never going to get another chance like this again. I could be the *only* human scientist *ever* to have this opportunity."

Yeah, she understood. It was that impulse that had driven her to rent a hover sled and set out over the frozen plains to discover the villages at the Murrun lakes.

"I'm...ninety-five percent certain this will work," Ben continued. "And if you could sedate the guards, you wouldn't be in danger of getting overpowered. Adriana, you're in good physical shape, but there's just no way you're a match for a fully grown Rendian soldier. I'm sorry."

Steven nodded at that. "He's not wrong. It's why I don't want you to go through with this plan. Even if the queen could incapacitate one of the guards, the other could seriously hurt you or sound the alarm before you kicked him in the nuts and stole his spear to stun him."

For a moment, everyone stared at Ben, pondering this.

Then Taron stepped forward. "I'll do it."

Ben glanced up, hope lighting his face. "Really?"

"Taron," Kol warned. "Don't be stupid."

"You heard him. This might give her a fighting chance. We only have one shot at this, brother, and if this adrenimine can knock out a warrior, Adriana and Zeema should be armed with it."

"*Adrenaline*," Ben corrected, earning himself a ferocious growl from Lhett.

"Do you have enough of it with you?" Adriana asked the doctor.

He nodded. "I have a box of two dozen EpiPens. Jean is severely allergic to bees, so we brought them as a precaution, but since I haven't seen a single bee on Rendu..."

Adriana looked at Mika, who shook her head. "No bees here. What plants they have are pollinated by these amazing moths..." She flushed, realizing everyone was grinning at her. "Which isn't the point here, sorry."

"We can spare a couple of EpiPens," Ben concluded. "I can get one right now."

"Do it," Taron commanded.

The doctor scampered out of the room, and Adriana turned to her tall alien, taking his hands in hers.

"Are you sure about this?" she asked quietly, trying to ignore everyone else. She was holding hands with her man, and she would *not* be ashamed of it. The cat was out of the bag anyway—Taron was holding on to her just as tightly.

"No," he murmured. "But I'll help you in any way I can. It will kill me to remain outside while you go in there alone."

"I know. But I won't be alone." She nodded at Mika and Hanne, then at Steven, who was pretending not to be listening to their conversation but now nodded enthusiastically. "We'll make this work, Taron."

He sighed and wrapped his large arms around her. She ended up smushed against his broad chest, breathing in his clean, minty scent. It calmed her senses and instilled a sense of tranquility inside her. She understood with sudden clarity what Taron had meant about *peace* being the foundation of a long-lasting relationship.

Then Ben returned with a handful of bright yellow EpiPens. "Here we go," he said, passing one to Taron.

Adriana eyed him skeptically. "Okay, but are we sure epinephrine won't harm him? Is there a way to...inject him with a smaller dose or something?"

Ben pursed his lips. "I mean...this *is* the first clinical trial. Ideally, if this was a real scientific experiment, we'd be doing months of testing in advance, then move to animals..."

Mika hissed, letting loose a string of expletives so vile, everyone flinched. Kol put a calming hand on her shoulder, but she shrugged it off. "Animal testing should be outlawed."

But Ben merely gave her a bored look, as though he'd heard this argument a hundred times before. "Would you rather have experimental new drugs tested on human subjects?"

Adriana wasn't sure she liked the Dutch doctor very much, but if his theory worked...

"So you can't say for certain it won't kill him?" Lhett summed up, arms crossed over his chest, his skin back to a pale blue.

"No, but I'm very optimistic."

At that moment, Taron crumpled to the floor beside her.

19

Adriana

THE ROOM ERUPTED WITH EXCLAMATIONS, but Adriana stood frozen to the spot. She took in the discarded EpiPen that rolled from Taron's hand, noted his slightly open lids, behind which only white showed.

Oh fuck. She dropped to her knees beside him, cradling his head, and searched for his pulse beneath his jaw. For one terrifying, endless moment, she didn't feel anything—and he was cold, so damn cold—but then her fingers came to rest on his vein. And there it was, Taron's heartbeat, slow, strong, and steady, as though he was deeply asleep.

Next to her, Ben was checking Taron's vitals, taking his blood pressure and shining a light into his eyes. He rattled off numbers to Kol and Lhett, who stood over their younger brother, confirming that he was, in fact, perfectly okay—but unconscious.

"Idiot," Lhett murmured, finally leaning back against the wall.

"How did he even know what to do?" Kol asked and gingerly picked up the EpiPen.

Ben sighed, removed his stethoscope, and stood. "The instructions come with pictures exactly for this purpose. EpiPens are very easy to use, even by children."

Adriana looked down at her alien. He'd made his decision and acted on it while the rest of them had been squabbling about details he'd deemed unimportant. And now here he was, laid out flat on the floor. She'd have a serious talk with him later—he should have at least lain on the bed before sticking himself in the leg. He could have hurt his head falling.

But the truth was, he'd done a very brave thing that they required of him—and she suspected that this was Taron at his core. Just as he'd come racing after her in the snowstorm, just as he'd killed those vile soldiers, this was who he was inside: a deeply honorable, brave man.

She smoothed his long white hair away from his forehead and pressed a kiss to his temple. He didn't even stir, but his cool breath caressed her cheek.

Adriana straightened and caught Hanne's gaze. Her friend smiled at her, a little wistful, a little sad, as if she already knew what decision Adriana had made. Tears prickled behind her eyes, and she blinked fast to keep her emotions under control. Saying goodbye to Mika and Hanne would be hard, perhaps harder than her farewell from her parents had been.

Minutes passed with no change, the members of their fledgling conspiracy team pensive and quiet. They agreed they wouldn't let the other members of the human team know about the plan—the fewer people knew about it, the less chance there was of someone behaving suspiciously. They didn't need Graham or the rest of the scientists for the execution of their plan.

Then, twenty-five minutes after he collapsed, Taron stirred from his slumber. His eyelids twitched first, then his leg, and he came awake slowly, mumbling something. Adriana stroked his cheek, and he leaned into her warmth, then grabbed her and dragged her down to lie with him as if on instinct. The rest of the crew chuckled while Adriana blushed and tried to wriggle free, but Taron wouldn't let go.

Mika hopped to her feet, took Kol's sleeve, and tugged him through the door. "Call us when he, uh, wakes up," she said and inclined her head to show the others that they should follow.

They all trooped out, and Ben called through the closing door that she should keep an eye on Taron until he fully recovered.

The moment the door closed behind them, Taron's eyes popped open, sky blue and clear.

Adriana gasped. "Have you been awake this whole time?"

He chuckled, running a palm down her back to grasp her ass. "No, but this is a nice way to wake up."

She squirmed under his touch; the rica leather of her pants was warm, but not very thick, and she felt every touch of his clever fingers.

"How much time do we have?" Taron murmured into her ear, then flicked his cold tongue over it.

Adriana shuddered at the sensation. "I don't know. The dinner is in less than three hours, and we need to... *Oh!*"

Taron worked his hand under her thermal shirt and pinched her nipple, so hard the pain of it pulsed through her nervous system before it dissolved into heady pleasure.

"Then I better make you come fast," her alien said, standing with a grace that shouldn't have been possible with a body so large and muscular as his.

Adriana scrambled to her feet, wondering if she should lock the door, but she didn't make it that far. Taron grabbed her, swung her around, and pressed her back to the black obsidian wall. It was warm to the touch behind her back, smooth as glass. She lifted her face to receive Taron's kiss, opened herself up to him, and gave him everything she had.

Within moments, their clothes lay discarded on the floor; she hopped up, wrapping her legs around his waist, while he supported her full weight with his palms. Without warning, he plunged deep inside her, sliding into her slick core, sheathing his thick, cold cock to the hilt.

Adriana threw her head back and moaned his name. Taron fucked her with shallow, powerful strokes, each one hitting the spot that had her seeing stars. She clung to his shoulders at first, but the moment she realized he was strong enough to hold her without her help, she let her hands roam over his back, feeling the spiky ridges of his spine.

Taron shouted in pleasure, his hips snapping forward. "Ah, fuck, do that again," he begged, then caught her mouth in another brutal, life-changing kiss.

Adriana found a spike on his upper back, smoothing her fingers over the skin-covered bump, and Taron dropped his head to her shoulder on a helpless moan.

He moved his hips faster, almost frantic in his need. He held her so tightly, his fingers would leave bruises on her thighs, but every time he hit the end of her, Adriana panted, her need coiling inside her like a spring.

"Is this what you like?" she muttered in his ear, playing with his reactions. "Tomorrow, after all this is over, I'll put you on your stomach and lick you all over until you come just from this," she promised.

Taron growled, all his restraint gone. He was a savage, ravaging her body with pleasure, pinching her nipples until Adriana couldn't breathe, fucking her long and hard. Her sweat-slicked back slid up and down the shiny wall with his every thrust.

On another wild, relentless stroke, she shattered, white light blinding her. A scream tore itself from her throat, and the force of her pleasure remade her world.

She gripped the spikes on his back with both hands, squeezing. Taron's eyes flew open, shock written all over his features the second before he came, and he bucked inside her time and time again, prolonging her orgasm.

Finally, the pulsing waves quieted, and Taron gently let her down on the floor. She swayed, so he put his arm out to steady her, always careful.

"Are you all right?" he murmured.

Adriana nodded, then wrapped her arms around his strong middle and lay her cheek on his chest to listen to his heartbeat. It didn't matter what he called the emotions—she knew what he felt for her was just as intense as her own feelings for him. She'd told him she loved him already but she didn't need him to repeat the words back to her. His actions spoke so much louder.

The moment stretched, the sounds of the palace rushing in around them, muted but present. Adriana stifled a yawn, wishing she could take a nap before dinner, but they didn't have the time: they needed to prepare for the evening.

"Do you really think it will work?" she asked, mentally going through all the steps of the plan. It was simple and imperfect but would serve its purpose.

Taron's faraway gaze told her he was considering all angles. "Provided the engineer does his work, yes." His arms tightened around her.

Adriana looked up to him. "Jean will find a way. But I want to thank you."

"What for?" asked Taron.

His blue gaze met hers, cool and collected—but Adriana heard the thrum of his heartbeat, still racing from their incredible interlude.

"For coming to save me. And for going along with this plan. I know it's not easy for you to trust us. But we won't let you down."

He hummed and put his chin on top of her head. "I trust *you*, Earthling. I'm not so sure about your teammates. But if you trust them..."

"I'd trust Mika and Hanne with my life," she said, echoing what he'd said about his brothers that first morning on Rendu. The two women were more sisters than mere friends to her; their shared adventure had tied them together in ways she hadn't expected. "And I'm certain Steven, Ben, and Jean will do what's required. Nobody else knows about the plan."

Taron sighed. "All right. Get dressed, then. We've got work to do."

They found Kol and Lhett in the mess hall, where they were eating a late lunch, apparently fueling up for the evening. Taron joined them, and they demolished an entire rack of rica ribs, as well as a mountain of soft, white rolls that quickly became Adriana's new favorite food on Rendu.

Taron insisted she'd need the calories for completing the plan.

"I'm going to dinner, remember?" she asked as she accepted a buttered roll from him.

"You won't be able to eat anything. You'll be too busy waiting for the perfect moment to implement the plan."

He piled more food on her plate—she suspected feeding her was somehow culturally significant to him, because he watched her like a hawk and offered her a jar of a tangy yellow spread that turned out to be caviar of some sort. She ate the food as she didn't want to hurt his feelings, but also because he was right. Even though she could barely force down the second roll, she knew Rendian cold sucked up all the energy she had—and if everything went according to plan, she would be spending time outside tonight after dark.

Lhett was the first to finish; he glowered at the rest of them until they hurried up and put away their trays. Then they all walked to Hanne's room—apparently that was the designated meeting space. But it was Mika who opened the door and put a finger to her lips. Hanne was fast asleep on the bed, her long blonde hair spilled all over the pillow.

Lhett stood at the threshold, staring at her. For a moment, an expression of such intense longing passed over his face, and Adriana turned away because it felt like an intrusion of privacy to witness it.

Then the eldest Naals brother cleared his throat. "She's, uh, she's tired. Always watching those stars. I'll..." He glanced at Taron, who nodded in understanding.

Lhett remained behind, keeping vigil over Hanne's sleeping form—they could afford to let her rest for an hour—while the rest of them went to find Jean.

The Canadian engineer was visibly exhausted and didn't say a word to them. He stood aside to let them enter his room and closed the door behind them. Lieutenant Anilla was slumped in the only chair, her face flushed blue. The metal collar around her neck looked dirty, as though they'd smeared it with tar.

"Have you figured it out?" Kol asked Jean, motioning at the collar.

Jean's expression was closed off and serious as he replied, "I have found a way to keep the queen from getting electrocuted. The entire collar will need to be coated in epoxy resin."

"That's amazing," Adriana exclaimed, clapping Jean on the shoulder. "I knew you could do it."

He pursed his lips, staring at the lieutenant for a long moment. "Yes, but at what cost?"

The beautiful soldier laughed hoarsely. "I volunteered, remember? Now get this thing off me."

Jean stepped forward immediately and unlocked the collar. Adriana didn't miss how he pressed his fingers against the lieutenant's cheek in a soft, lingering touch—or that she didn't seem to mind. It wasn't just her relationship with Taron that was getting increasingly complicated.

"Can't we use that key to unlock the queen's collar?" Mika's clear voice pierced the silence.

"Each collar's lock is different," Taron explained to her. "And the regent has the key to Zeema's."

"Of course." Mika rolled her eyes in frustration. "Why would anything ever be easy?"

Kol nudged her. "Your role tonight won't be complicated. You just need to keep the regent occupied."

Mika snorted. "Not a problem. I can talk about vissnae harvesting for ages."

Adriana had to stifle a laugh at Kol's shocked face. He probably didn't believe Mika could charm the evil usurper by prattling on about alien squid, and she privately agreed. But she also believed in Mika's determination—her friend would figure it out. And she'd have Hanne by her side to help her, though their Danish colleague was far less chatty.

Lieutenant Anilla sighed, stretching her back like a cat, and got to her feet. She wobbled and put a hand to the wall to steady herself. "Excuse me," she said. "I need to go find a shirt that will cover up this gunk." She pointed at the black smudges left all over her neck, touched Jean's hand for the briefest moment, and left.

The engineer stared after her, as though he wanted nothing more than to follow.

"She'll be fine," Taron said quietly. "I've served with her for a decade—she's tough."

Jean seemed to snap out of it. "Yes, of course. I need to explain to you how this works."

He picked up the collar and a translucent tube half filled with a black resin. Then he turned to Taron.

But Taron merely shook his head and pointed at Adriana. Jean looked from one to the other with wide, shocked eyes.

"You cannot be serious," he hissed, the words laced with anger that was so uncharacteristic of him. "You can't send *her* to do your work."

Adriana flinched. "Not this again," she grumbled. "We've gone over the plan a hundred times. There's *no way* Taron—or any other Rendian, for that matter—can get close enough to the queen to help her." She held out her hand. "Now stop worrying about me and show me how this works."

20

Taron

HE FOLLOWED Adriana to her room, where she would prepare for the evening. She hid the small tube of insulating resin inside her waistband and covered it with her shirt—but she would need to find a different place to carry it into the royal dining hall. All guests would be searched before dinner.

The door closed behind them, and Taron leaned against it, letting out a long breath. "I need to talk to you about something."

The question had been needling him ever since he realized she might be carrying his child. The thought, while terrifying, ignited a strange nugget of warmth inside his chest.

"Mm?" she murmured, kneeling on the floor and digging through one of her drawers. She pulled out a beautiful red dress she must have brought from Earth. "What do you think?" she asked. She got to her feet and held the dress in front of her. "I brought it with me because the human delegation was supposed to meet the king."

Taron smiled sadly. "You would have impressed him in that dress. He would have liked you."

Adriana stepped over to him and touched his cheek. "I'm sorry. I know you haven't been given time to mourn him yet."

He hung his head. "I'll mourn him when this is done." *When the regent is dead.* He didn't want to voice the thought, but there was no way this would end any other way. He cleared his throat and added, "I have a different question to ask you."

She lifted her dark eyebrows, her brown gaze focused on him. Whenever she stared at him like this, he knew he had her full attention. His human didn't do anything by halves.

"Is it possible that you're pregnant with our child?" he said. His voice turned rough, so the words were harsher than he'd planned, but he didn't see a point in waiting.

Adriana blinked. Had she really not thought about this?

But then she slowly shook her head. "Not yet," she whispered. "At least I'm pretty sure. I've got protection. Bringing a baby into this mess wouldn't be responsible, don't you think?"

He agreed—and yet... "Will you want to? Eventually?"

She clasped his face in her warm palms, which always seemed to foretell something significant she had to say. "Yes. I'm not sure if it'll even work, but I would love to try."

Taron kissed her, failing to form the words that would express what he was feeling. He'd never been good with words. So he would show her with his body instead, worship her until she gasped his name.

But Adriana pulled away. "We can't." When he tried to kiss her again, she added, "Taron. I need to shower and change."

He let her go, pressing himself back against the door. "I'll wait here."

There was no chance he was letting her out of his sight before it was absolutely necessary. Tonight, they would challenge the regent and try to save the queen. Tonight, everything would change.

How, he wasn't sure—their plan was solid, but there were so many variables to it, so many points where it could go massively, horribly wrong. It spoke to their desperation that they'd decided to go ahead with it; Lhett was likely pulling his hair out from worry.

Taron chose not to think about it. They could do nothing but follow the steps, one after the other, and hope everything fell into place.

He waited for Adriana to get ready. He didn't need to change—he and his brothers would soon be going out into the city, first to the barracks to see which soldiers would still follow their former general into battle. It was time for the nation to pick sides—even though the resulting fight might become a civil war.

But he had to hope, he had to believe that his people would rally behind their rightful leader, even if she was too young to legally take the throne.

They couldn't have done this before—not without having a plan to save Zeema from torture. A single whisper of a planned uprising in the regent's ear, brought by one of his many paid spies around the city, would have meant possible death for the queen. But with the human engineer's solution, they had a fighting chance.

But first, he'd need to play his role in the little charade

Mika had thought of: something to lend credibility to the planned events.

The bathroom door opened, curls of steam escaping into the room. Taron straightened and stretched; he hadn't realized how much time had passed. A glance at his tablet told him Adriana had less than an hour to present herself in the palace's reception hall.

She stepped out of the bathroom, and Taron could only stare. The soft knit dress hugged her curves but covered her arms. It showed a hint of her cleavage, tempting Taron to hook his finger in her collar and tug it lower.

"Um, I forgot my earrings," she announced. "But I need another minute."

She grabbed something silvery off her nightstand—he'd never seen her wear any ornaments in her ears before, so he was curious to see what they looked like—and she turned back toward the bathroom.

Taron nearly swallowed his tongue.

The back of the dress was missing. It simply wasn't there—and neither was anything else. It exposed most of Adriana's spine, making it perfectly clear she wasn't wearing anything underneath.

Taron growled, then closed in on her. Now he'd have to spend the entire evening not only worrying about her but painfully hard and aching.

Adriana seemed oblivious to him—she stood in front of the bathroom mirror with her mouth full of pins and was busy knotting her hair into some elaborate formation that would make a sailor proud. Two brown sticks were poking out of it. Taron wasn't sure whether they counted as weapons or decoration.

"I'm hiding the tube in here," she explained.

Taron looked more closely and saw she was entirely

serious—only the cap of the tube was visible in the twist of hair, and with several deft loops, she covered even that. The tube wasn't that heavy, but if her hair unraveled...

Adriana closed her eyes and sprayed her head with some sort of mist. Taron coughed, waving his hand to dissipate it.

"Sorry," she murmured. "It'll help hold it in."

Taron touched her exposed neck lightly with his fingertips. She stilled, meeting his gaze in the mirror, and he was transported back into that dressing room—was it really only a month ago? He traced his fingers down her spine and listened for any change in her breathing. *Ah, there it is.* The telltale hitch, a tiny gasp that spoke louder than if she'd shouted out loud.

Goose bumps formed on her smooth skin, and Taron leaned in to press a soft, barely there kiss to her shoulder.

Still holding his gaze, she took out a stick of red pigment and painted her lips.

Hmm. If she was still capable of fine motor skills, he was doing something wrong.

With his other hand, he reached lower, where the hem of her dress touched the backs of her knees. Ever so slowly, he lifted the fabric, keeping contact with the warm skin of her thigh.

She was breathing faster now, but she didn't tell him to stop. No, her gaze now held a hint of challenge, and she put one silver stud in her earlobe.

Taron grinned at her over her shoulder, then licked her neck, simultaneously dragging his palm to the inside of her thigh, higher and higher...

He cursed violently, his cock throbbing.

Adriana wasn't wearing underwear.

Her knowing gaze, the sensual twist of her red-painted lips—it was too much.

"Is your hair done?" he growled, running rough fingers through the wetness between her legs.

She was ready for him, and a whimper escaped her when he found her slick clit.

"Yes." She turned around in his arms. "Don't you dare ruin it. Or my makeup. I spent too long trying to get it perfect for tonight."

"You're already perfect." The words flew from his mouth, and Taron knew they were the truest he'd ever spoken. At her startled gaze, he took her chin, but instead of fusing his lips to hers, which was what he wanted to do, he tipped her head to the side and kissed her neck. She'd covered the purple kiss-bruises somehow, so he took care not to smudge her paint. Nibbling his way down to her shoulder, then back again to her ear, he whispered, "I don't need to ruin your hair to fuck you."

Her gasp hit him straight in the gut, so scandalized but so eager. "Show me," she murmured.

Taron didn't waste any time. Grabbing her waist, he hauled her out the bathroom, to her bed, where he released her with a simple order, "Get on your hands and knees."

Adriana's eyes darkened, her red mouth half open with desire. She obeyed, climbing onto the bed, clearly thinking he would follow her, but he stopped her advance with a hand to her hip.

"No. Here, at the edge."

Where he could stand behind her, have her poised before him like an offering. He lifted the hem of her dress, slowly, until she was bare, the fabric scrunched up around her waist.

Adriana glanced over her shoulder. "I want you now, Taron."

"Patience," he murmured, offering her a feral grin, trying to hold back when all he wanted was to bury himself inside her and fuck her until her arms gave out. "I need to make sure..."

Dipping his fingers inside her core, he had her panting in seconds, stretching her, preparing her, because he couldn't be gentle tonight. Not when his entire body was screaming to claim, to take, to make her his. Gentle was the furthest thing from his mind, the peace he'd spoken about replaced by a need so powerful, a want so violent, his chest felt like iron bands closed around it. Every time he was near her, he could barely breathe for the intensity of it. Every time she came on his cock, he thanked the skies that he'd found her.

She hadn't spoken those fateful words since their return to the capital, and he wanted to wring them from her—so the roaring beast inside him would relent. So he could tell her the same.

"Please," she begged, her palms dragging over the sheets in restless, frantic motions. "Please, Taron!"

Her hips undulated under his touch, and he realized she was close. He knew her body now, knew what she liked, what had her screaming his name. So he reached down and pinched her clit between his fingers, rolling the tiny bud again and again, and she came on his hand, moaning, her arms trembling under her.

Taron couldn't wait any longer. Undoing the laces on his pants, he dropped them and his underwear, fisted his cock, and held her hips steady with his other hand. Then he plunged inside her, through the last ripples of her orgasm, into the wet, addictive heat of her. He pulled back and nearly slipped out of her, then thrust forward again, deeper this time.

Adriana went to her elbows, as if she was no longer capable of supporting her body, but when she looked over her shoulder at him, she growled, "Harder."

Taron would have laughed if he had any breath left in his lungs. She was perfect, the ideal match for him. She took his cock like she was made to do it, but always kept him on his guard. Life would never be boring with her.

"Say it," he commanded, slamming into her. Her tight heat surrounded him, whipping his desire into a frenzy. He moved above her and leaned over to grab one full breast in his palm. "Say it, and I'll make you come again."

"Taron," she whimpered, "I..."

He put his lips to her ear. "I want to hear it."

He squeezed her breast, finding her nipple with such ease—he reveled in the fact that he would have years, even *decades*, to explore everything that brought her pleasure.

"I love you," she screamed, her voice echoing from the shining black walls surrounding them. "Taron, I love you."

He slid his hand down to her core, found her little knot of nerves, and rubbed two fingers over it in slow, calculated circles. Her body tensed beneath his, and he put on more pressure, but decreased the pace of his thrusts. He was close yet didn't want to blow before he brought her over once more, just to show her how much he...

She snuck a hand beneath them, reaching below, and took hold of his balls. Taron's eyes rolled back, and his hips jerked forward. The sensation wasn't as strong as with his spine spikes but... "Fuck!" he roared, arching over her, too close to coming.

Adriana's breathless laugh caressed his senses. "Don't you dare slow down," she ordered and gave his balls a tug.

And Taron was done. His discipline disappeared, his resolve went down the drain; all that remained was the addictive heat he was buried in, the warm fingers closing on his balls, and Adriana's voice ringing in his ears.

"Faster, Taron. Ah, I love you."

He could barely control himself for long enough to make sure she found her orgasm, undulating under him. Then he slammed into her one more time and came so hard, he had to catch himself on the bed so he didn't squash Adriana. The tremors of his pleasure rolled through his body, recalibrating his cells so they would only ever point in her direction. He would always know where she was, always feel her absence when she was away.

Withdrawing from her, he helped her clean up—he didn't want to mess up her beautiful dress—then gathered her in his lap.

"I love you. Will you stay?" he murmured against her ear, nuzzling along the fragrant skin of her neck.

The words were foreign on his tongue, but there was no doubt in his mind that they were correct. He'd never thought it possible that the peace she gave him just by being near would unite with his lust into this *love*, and yet...

She nodded but didn't say a word, so he lifted his head to look at her.

Water leaked silently from the corners of her eyes.

"Ah, little Earthling, don't be sad." He kissed away the salty, bitter liquid. "It's going to be all right."

She sniffed and shook her head, then gave him the most brilliant smile. "I'm not crying because I'm sad. I'm happy. I didn't think you'd..." She hiccupped and twisted in his lap until she found a tissue to blow her nose. "I'm just happy."

Taron rubbed his hand over his eyes. "So you also do this when you're not sad? How do I know what's going on?"

She patted his arm. "You'll learn. You'll have all the time in the world to figure it out."

At this, Taron's thoughts cleared enough to remember the dinner. "I will if everything goes well tonight." He kissed her despite her warning to stay away from her makeup. "I hate that I won't be there to protect you."

She kissed him back, her warm tongue caressing his, easing some of his worry. Then she hopped off his lap and straightened her dress. "It'll be over before you know it. And tomorrow, you'll be free to resume your position on your ship and continue doing what you do best."

Taron tied his pants and frowned at her. "Do you think I'd ask you to stay on Rendu for me, then fly away on missions for months at a time?"

The vulnerable look in Adriana's eyes expressed that was exactly what she'd thought.

"And yet you decided to stay?" he added.

She shrugged. "I figured spending even short periods of time with you would be worth it. I'd be like a sailor's wife, except you'd be sailing among the stars." Her grin told him she was trying to be brave, but her hands were tightly clasped in front of her.

"Adriana," he murmured. He stepped closer and cupped her cheeks with his palms, turning her face up so she had to look him in the eyes. "I won't leave you. I'll find another way to provide for us. For our family, if we'll ever be blessed enough to have it."

"Stop it," she wailed, "I can't keep crying. I don't have time to fix my makeup."

He chuckled and let her go. "We'll talk about this tonight," he promised. "After you've returned to me and the queen is saved."

She paled a little at that but nodded. "It's nearly time to go."

Taron kissed her once more, inhaling the scent of her, and caressed her warm, supple body. "You'll do great. At least now you can be sure your hair will really hold the tube," he joked.

He needed her relaxed, or her nervous glances and fidgeting would give away their plan. She wasn't a soldier or a trained operative, just a very brave, smart woman who'd volunteered to help his people without question. He loved her so much, it physically hurt him to let her out of his sight.

But his words had had the desired effect.

She laughed, tentatively poking the knot of hair on the back of her head. "Now we just have to sell our little performance. Are you ready?"

Taron swatted her ass as she turned to leave the room. "What's a little pain compared to saving a planet?"

21

Adriana

"SHOW TIME," she whispered and rolled back her shoulders. She knew full well that the dress she was wearing showed off her curves to their best advantage, and she wasn't above using them to distract the guards into thinking she was just a harmless human.

Taron had left her in the mess hall; she would see him again, briefly, in just a couple of minutes, but they couldn't be seen arriving together or their plan wouldn't work. She was afraid of going to dinner without him—or without the rest of their friendly Rendian guards—but they all agreed that the regent couldn't risk attacking any of them while the representatives from the Intergalactic Trade Association were present. He needed the delegates to remain happy and convinced that everything on Rendu was just peachy, despite the fact that he murdered the king.

Adriana greeted the two soldiers stationed at the entrance to the great reception hall. She didn't know them; they were likely members of the regent's private force. Then she spotted Hanne and Mika already waiting there with Ben.

"Hi," she greeted them. "You both look gorgeous!" She pitched her voice higher on purpose so the guards would have no trouble listening in to their conversation.

Her friends returned the exclamations, praising her dress, and they chatted animatedly—or at least she and Mika did, while Hanne tried her best not to look too nervous. Adriana hoped that the Rendians would assume the astrophysicist was just nervous because she would soon be meeting the queen and the regent.

Other members of the human team arrived, Graham leering unpleasantly at Mika, who flipped him the finger while the guards weren't watching. Their colleagues, everyone from the broad-shouldered Jean to the tiny Damini, a botanist from India, had put on their Sunday best, resulting in a stunning array of formal wear.

"But where's Steven?" Adriana exclaimed loudly, drawing the guard's attention like they'd planned.

"Sick as a dog," Ben replied on cue. "I've been to see him, and he won't be leaving his bathroom anytime soon. I left him a powder to help with the diarrhea and I'll check on him after dinner."

One of the guards snickered quietly as the members of their team who weren't in on the plan expressed surprise and worry that the bug Adriana had supposedly caught might be contagious. *Perfect.*

Now all she needed to do was wait for Taron...

He came bounding down the narrow corridor a minute

later, pushing a passing Rendian out of the way so the man's load of tall glasses tipped over and shattered on the floor with a loud crash. This wasn't part of the plan, but Adriana had to cheer Taron's resourcefulness—the more witnesses they gathered for this event, the better.

"Adriana," Taron bellowed, stopping three feet from her and glowering down, his expression fierce.

If she didn't know him, she would have been scared—he was every inch the wild Rendian warrior, ready to tear someone limb from limb, and all his ire was focused on her.

"What?" she snapped. "I thought I told you to stay away from me."

A feminine gasp sounded behind her; Mika was enjoying her role far too much. But a clatter of boots on the stone floor also told her more Rendians had joined the show.

Taron stepped closer. "Do you want to explain why your little human toy is sick, just as you were?" he growled.

"It's none of your business," she retorted, glaring at him. *Wow, we're pretty good at this.* She had to stifle a nervous giggle—and from the way Taron's eyes crinkled in the corners, she thought he recognized that she was on the verge of a panicked laughing attack.

"It is my business if you're fucking—"

Adriana slapped him across the face, really putting her weight into the blow.

They'd discussed it when formulating the plan, and Lhett had claimed that the guards would know a faked blow from a real one. "Just punch him," he'd advised her. "He'll live."

Taron had shrugged and agreed. The Naals brothers had a funny way of showing affection to each other.

Now Taron's head snapped to the side—he might have overplayed the reaction a little bit, but no one seemed to care: they were all staring at them with open mouths. Taron turned a deep blue, yet his cheek remained pale with the outline of her hand imprinted on it. *Strange.* She was instantly sorry for the blow, but much as she wanted to throw her arms around him and kiss the bruise better, she knew that would defeat the purpose.

"Guards," a bored voice called from behind her. "Restrain him."

Adriana whirled around and came face to face with Regent Yaroh ad Gilmar, the bastard who'd killed his king and enslaved the young queen.

"Your Highness," she intoned, dropping into a quick curtsy and straightening.

His gaze cut to her. "Dr. Ribeiro, I presume. Pleased to meet you."

He took her hand and brushed his cold lips over her knuckles. Unlike Taron's cool touch, the regent's had her shivering in revulsion.

She covered the reaction and smiled at him. "Please, call me Adriana."

The man smirked—he was handsome, as good-looking as any Rendian she'd seen in the streets. He was tall and broad, and Adriana didn't have trouble imagining he was very skilled at convincing others to do things his way. But there was a cruel slant to his lips, and his pale-blue eyes were icy cold, without a flicker of kindness.

Behind her, two guards seized Taron, just as they'd expected. He struggled a little, but they pointed the ends of their spears at his chest, and he quieted.

"Take him to a cell to cool off," the regent instructed.

He was speaking in a raised voice, Adriana realized, for the benefit of the delegates from the Intergalactic Trade Association who stood behind him. "We take our human visitors' safety very seriously."

Taron hung his head and allowed the guards to escort him down the corridor. Adriana knew he would deal with them—stun them, not kill them; they'd agreed on keeping casualties to the minimum—the moment they turned the corner. Two less soldiers to guard the reception hall, and two less for the rest of their crew to deal with if the plan went to hell.

"Come, appetizers will be served in a minute," the regent called, ushering the delegates into the hall.

Adriana and her teammates followed behind them. The guards searched them at the door, but beyond waving their tablets at them, they didn't perform any full-body searches. Hanne caught Adriana's hand, giving it a quick squeeze, then released her and fell into step with Jean. They all had their roles to play.

And hers was to get roaring drunk at the dinner party.

"I mean, why can't he just *accept* that I'm not a one-man woman?" she slurred, sloshing some of the purple wine from her goblet. The word *accept* came out with a very deliberate lisp, and she might have spit a little on poor Queen Zeema, who was staring at her with wide eyes.

Adriana wasn't drunk. In fact, she'd had maybe two sips of the drink and had spilled the rest of each glassful onto a cushion she kicked under the table the moment they arrived in the formal dining room.

The chamber was enormous, with a black vaulted ceiling that soared thirty feet in the air above their heads, and was decorated with lavish, imported silks. Taron had told her the regent had had it redesigned as soon as he took control over the throne, likely so he could showcase his wealth to delegations such as the one sitting with them at the table.

To Adriana, the general effect seemed more like a French boudoir than a stately dining room, but what did she know about intergalactic trade negotiations?

The three greenish aliens currently sitting on a low divan at the other end of the table certainly looked impressed. Adriana assumed the tentacles waving around their heads were a sign of happiness, not alarm. Their chattering, high-pitched voices mingled with the talk of the human delegation and the lower voices of the Rendian courtiers. There were seven of those at the table, more than they'd expected—these were representatives of the Rendian noble houses to whom the death of their king hadn't presented a particular problem. They'd simply allied themselves with whoever held the power at the moment.

Adriana wished she could glare at them for being so callous—Queen Zeema was sitting at the table, rigid under the weight of their stares. Which was why Adriana had drawn her into the conversation. She would have loved to talk to the queen on a normal occasion, but for the time being, she needed to appear as drunk as possible.

She glanced around the table. Nobody was watching her; they'd all dismissed her as a crass, low-life human who couldn't hold her drink. Now she slipped her goblet beneath the tablecloth and spilled her wine again.

She glanced up to find Zeema watching, her mouth

parted in surprise. Adriana winked at her and chanced a low whisper, "Go to the bathroom."

The young queen didn't react. Instead, she picked up her goblet of water and drank deeply, motioning to a waiting servant to refill it soon after. She conversed with the regent, who was seated on her right side, and ate more food. Adriana didn't dare talk to her again but loudly demanded more wine instead.

On the regent's other side, Mika was explaining about the mating habit of ferrets. Ben was helping her distract the regent by laughing loudly at her every word while Graham glared angrily at the Dutch doctor. She hoped the soldier wouldn't cause a scene.

"Do you think we could have some music?" Hanne inquired gently, addressing the noblewoman next to her. "At human parties, it's usual to have some sort of musical entertainment."

Kol had assured them that the Rendians would not want to be outdone by humans, especially in front of their important guests—not when it came to throwing a good party. A troupe of musicians was soon brought forward, and they struck up a tune that added to the echoing noise of the chamber. Adriana breathed a sigh of relief.

Her friend shifted in her seat, and then Adriana felt a brush of something against her leg. She extended her arm under the table and accepted the EpiPen Hanne had smuggled into the room—they'd decided it would be far too dangerous for Adriana to carry everything they needed for the plan to work. She now tucked the injection device into her boot, waiting for the second to come her way.

A few minutes later, Ben got up to admire the view from one of the windows, asking the woman seated beside him to point out the city's landmarks.

"So beautiful," he exclaimed as he dropped the other EpiPen on the cushion next to Adriana's low chair.

She shuddered with relief. So far, so good. There were too many people in the room for the regent to keep track of them all, and the guards were posted at the entrances, not watching the guests. That would have tipped off the diplomats that something was amiss, and the regent was doing his best to assure them that the flow of platinum from Rendu would continue uninterrupted despite the recent political changes.

Adriana wished she could stick a fork in his eyeball and make that obnoxious smirk disappear from his face.

She would have to settle for saving the queen.

A small eternity passed before Zeema pushed back her chair and stood. The regent barely registered her movement, nodding at the two guards who stood nearby. They followed her closely, and Adriana found she hated the usurper even more. The poor young woman couldn't even go to the toilet on her own.

She waited a minute longer and pretended to gulp more wine. Then got to her feet, swaying slightly. "Oh my god," she gasped. "The room is spinning. Can someone point me in the direction of the bathroom?"

The nobles sneered at her in disgust, but one of the attendants indicated the far corner of the chamber, where Zeema had disappeared.

"Thanks," Adriana whispered loudly and stumbled her way toward the door.

She rounded the corner, passing out of their eyesight, but she didn't stop weaving. There was the first guard, standing in front of the bathroom door.

She tripped deliberately, catching herself just in time, and used the maneuver to pull an EpiPen from her boot, hiding it by pressing her arm to her side. It likely looked unnatural, but she hoped this Rendian wouldn't know what was 'natural' for drunk humans.

"Oh, hi," she crooned. "Aren't you a big guy."

"The bathroom is that way, madam," he replied, his voice clipped. He was young, not much older than the queen herself, and yet he'd chosen to follow Gilmar instead of standing with his young monarch. She was just debating where and how to stick him with the needle when a crash sounded from the bathroom.

The guard instantly jumped toward the door, Adriana close behind him. She flicked the cap off the EpiPen and aimed for the young man's neck. She was in luck—he hadn't activated his armor's helmet, so the needle sank right into his blue skin.

Adriana pressed down with her thumb, releasing the epinephrine into the guard's bloodstream. The man collapsed with a clatter, and his spear rolled away from him, toward Adriana. She picked it up gingerly, listening to the sounds from beyond the hallway. The music still played, and no running footsteps neared her, so she supposed the diversion had worked.

She eyed the weapon in her hand, hefting it. It wasn't heavy, but she'd had no training with it. She was passable with a gun—yet they had brought none of those to Rendu. Would she even know how to use the spear without hurting herself? She should have insisted on a lesson from Taron instead of allowing him to seduce her.

A second bump came from behind the closed door—she couldn't waste any more time. Gripping the spear in one hand and the EpiPen in the other, she took a deep breath and toed the door open.

The scene that greeted her shocked her into stopping.

The queen cowered in the corner while the other guard, a middle-aged Rendian in full armor, stood over her, prodding her with the tip of his spear.

No, not prodding—he wasn't actually touching her, though the spear was shooting out little bolts of electricity. Each one shocked Zeema like a taser, and if her whimpers were any indication, they hurt her. A lot.

"You think you're so special," the man muttered as he shot her twice, *zap, zap*. "Refusing to marry my son. Like you're better than him. You're nothing." *Zap.*

Adriana gasped. She couldn't help her reaction any more than she could stop breathing—and the sound seemed to echo in the empty bathroom, amplified by the sheer black walls.

"What?" The guard turned on his heels, gripping his spear tighter. "What are you doing here? Get out. This is none of your business."

Adriana pointed the spear at him. "You let her go!" Her voice shook—she hadn't expected the confrontation to unfold like this. She'd gotten lucky with the younger guard and had hoped she could surprise this one as well.

He stepped forward, menacing. "Where'd you get that spear? Aresh?" he called out, likely to the guard outside.

"He's down," Adriana told him. "And if you don't put aside your weapon, I'll take you out, too."

He laughed. The bastard actually *laughed* at her. That was what pissed her off the most. But the truth was, she had no idea how to wield the spear, and she didn't want to get shocked again. The first time at that snowy, empty village had hurt enough.

Behind the guard, Zeema struggled quietly to her feet, her glare murderous. She lifted her arm and made a 'gimme' motion with her fingers. Adriana blinked—did she want the spear?

The moment of confusion cost her. The guard stepped into her space, faster than she'd anticipated, and back-handed her across the face. It was an insult; she didn't even merit the use of his weapon.

Tears sprang into her eyes from the pain. *Fuck!* Any moment now, someone could pass by. They'd see the unconscious guard outside and raise the alarm.

Her vision cleared, and she tossed the weapon at the queen as best she could—it clattered on the floor beside her instead of landing in her outstretched arm.

"Shit." Adriana gritted her teeth and launched herself at the guard. If she could just prick him with the needle...

He blocked her advance with practiced ease and slapped her again. Adriana's mouth filled with blood, and she hoped he hadn't knocked a tooth loose. Though she would gladly pay a tooth if it meant getting out of here alive...which was looking less and less likely. This guard didn't seem worried about interstellar consequences. He was either too dumb or too cocky to understand what hurting Adriana might mean for him, but in that moment, his reasoning didn't matter. He could kill her in minutes.

He grabbed her by the shoulder, reaching back to deal her another vicious blow.

And the queen cut off his hand.

An arc of blue blood sprayed from the stump, painting the white marble sink and the mirrors. The guard seemed stunned, staring at it, then at the severed hand lying on the floor.

"Shit, oh shit," Adriana cursed, trying to hold back vomit. She stumbled away from the man.

Zeema kicked him in the ass, and he went sprawling on

the floor, his large body landing with a wet *thwack* on the bloody obsidian.

He yelled, and she kicked him in the face. Adriana flinched back from the ferocity of her glare, but the queen was doing what needed to be done: they couldn't allow him to scream.

This jolted her into motion—she dropped to her knees beside the soldier and jabbed the needle of the EpiPen into his cheek. He went limp instantly, his eyes rolling back. Zeema knelt next to him and took up his wrist. Adriana thought she might bind his stump, make a tourniquet, but the queen deactivated his armor with a press of her fingers. Then she lifted the spear and stabbed him right in the back.

The man didn't even twitch.

Adriana stared at the young woman, too shocked to speak.

The queen bared her teeth. "What, you think this was the first time he tortured me?"

Adriana shook her head, blinking tears of pain and terror from her eyes. "No. No, of course not. I'm sorry I couldn't help you sooner." She reached for her and put her hand on the queen's shoulder.

At that, Zeema dropped the spear, wrapped her arms around herself, and shook, her entire body racked with shudders. Adriana had no idea whether she was going into shock or suffering an aftereffect of her torture, but they needed to act fast.

She undid her hair, tucked the two decorative sticks inside her bra, and pulled out the tube Jean had prepared for her. "Here," she said. "Smear this all over your collar. It'll irritate your skin but it will insulate you from the electric current."

The queen looked at her with glassy eyes, uncomprehending, so Adriana took her hands.

"Please, you have to move. You'll get a chance to rest later, but right now, we need to make sure the regent can't hurt you anymore. Everything depends on that."

Zeema blinked once, twice, then slowly uncurled herself, took the tube, and stood in front of the mirror. Once Adriana was sure she understood what the process was, she ducked her head out of the bathroom and checked the corridor. Then she grabbed the young guard by the hands and dragged him into the room. Her progress was excruciatingly slow because of his weight, and she feared that at any moment, one of the guests would arrive or another guard would come to check what was taking the queen so long. They likely had only moments before their ruse was discovered.

Blue hands appeared beside hers, grabbing the guard. Zeema worked with Adriana to push and slide him all the way in and locked the door behind them. Then she returned to her task, and Adriana helped her reach the parts of the collar at the back.

A tap on the window scared them both; Zeema covered her scream with her resin-smeared hand and accidentally painted smudges on her face.

But it was only Steven on a hover sled, riding fifty feet above the icy ground below. Adriana jumped to open the window.

"Are you ready?" he asked, then took in Adriana's bruised face and a second later, the clearly dead guard on the floor. "What happened?"

"No time to explain." Adriana squeezed the last of the epoxy resin onto the queen's collar, patting it down over where she hoped the receiver was. This was it—their plan would either work or it wouldn't.

She passed Steven the two spears they'd liberated from the guards. The soldier stashed them at his side, nodding in thanks. Then Zeema clambered onto the high windowsill and took the short but dangerous leap into the sled.

The vehicle dipped a little, swerving away from the wall, and Steven caught the queen. He helped her settle— then tried to maneuver the sled back to the window.

The door behind Adriana crashed open.

A Rendian guard appeared on the threshold and yelled, "They're getting away!"

Adriana looked at the ledge, which was high enough that she couldn't easily scale it, then met Steven's gaze. "Go," she whispered.

He shook his head and extended his hands. "Come on, Adriana. Hurry!"

"Go," she screamed. "If you don't save the queen, we've failed. Go now, that's an order!"

She had no real authority over him, but Steven's face hardened, and he nodded. Then he flicked a button on the hover sled's control panel, took up the steering stick, and the vehicle dove into the night. The queen screamed as they sped away, telling him to return, but Adriana was pleased to see Steven wasn't listening.

A hand grabbed her shoulder, and she was spun roughly around.

The man facing her was none other than Regent Gilmar, surrounded by his personal guard.

"Where did they go?" he snarled.

Adriana remained silent. The regent cursed and pulled a small, shiny device from his pocket. With a vicious grin, he pressed a button.

"It won't work," Adriana told him. "She's free from you."

The regent glared at her, then pressed the button again and again. Adriana hoped to god that Jean's solution had worked—if it hadn't, the queen was likely writhing in excruciating pain at the moment.

"Find her," he ordered his guards, and they trooped out of the room, leaving her alone with him.

Even though she was facing a single man instead of six, a bead of cold sweat rolled down her back. He looked unhinged, and she wasn't sure to what lengths he'd go to secure his position.

"You think you can ruin me? That the little bitch you helped save was really necessary for my plan?" He spat at her feet. "And to think the Naals idiots are consorting with you. Filth."

Well. This was enlightening. The grand diplomat was less than charming in private. Adriana couldn't say she was surprised. She inched to the left, trying to go for the door, but Gilmar wasn't stupid, just enraged. He grabbed her by the front of her dress and tossed her into a corner, where she hit her head on the wall.

The room spun, and Adriana spit out blood—whether it was from that slap she'd received from the guard or this new injury, she didn't know, but she was *scared*. The sheer strength of this man was terrifying; he'd thrown her as though she weighed nothing. She knew Rendians were stronger than humans and she wasn't a very strong human to begin with. For the first time since they'd conceived this plan, she doubted her own sanity.

What was she doing, taking on an alien planet's politics? She should have kept her head down, let someone else take care of this mess.

But shame flooded her veins at that moment of doubt. She thought of Taron, who'd dropped everything to fly after her into enemy territory, right into a freaking ice storm. She thought of Queen Zeema, a girl too young to even take the throne, taking out the guard who had been torturing her. She thought of the empty villages she'd seen at the Murrun lakes.

She couldn't let this man win. When he came closer to strike her again, she fought like a wildcat, scratching his eyes, biting the hand with which he closed her mouth so her screams wouldn't reverberate around the bathroom.

But it didn't matter—he was too strong, and now she was on her back, and the regent's large hands closed around her throat. Black spots danced across her vision. She scratched against his forearms, but he was wearing armor under his courtier's clothes. He was crushing her windpipe...

"Sir, you need to see this."

A soldier appeared at the door, breaking the regent's concentration. He released Adriana, and she sucked in a painful, desperate breath. Curling up on her side, she whimpered, her throat raw, her vision blurry with tears. *Fuck*, getting nearly strangled hurt.

Gilmar kicked her, but the move was half-hearted at best and barely glanced off her shoulder; she covered her head with her arms and hoped that whatever it was, he'd be moved to go investigate.

"There's a transmission going, sir," the soldier said, his gray eyes wide. "It...appears to be broadcast nationwide."

The regent didn't even glance at her; he stalked out of the room, the soldier scrambling behind him.

Slowly, Adriana pushed to her hands and knees, though she nearly collapsed. She needed to get out of there. Her friends might be in danger, too—and she knew with a cold, bone-deep certainty, she would not survive if that psycho returned to finish what he'd started.

She crawled to the door and used the wall to get to her feet. Everything hurt—her jaw, her head, her throat, and a hundred other pains and bruises. But she was breathing, so that was a definite bonus. She would *not* be the first human to die on this strange, beautiful planet.

22

Taron

ADRIANA WAS NOT on the hover sled. The realization hit him in the chest with a concussive force the second he laid eyes on the approaching vehicle. She was not with Zeema and Steven, which meant a part of the plan had gone terribly wrong.

The rooftop in the lower city, where they'd agreed to meet, was dusted with snow, only his footsteps marring it. He'd been pacing back and forth for the past hour. As they'd agreed, he'd gotten rid of the two guards, then accompanied his brothers to the barracks, where they explained to the soldiers, in no uncertain terms, that the regent's rule would soon be coming to an end.

The two idiots who'd tried to run, probably to warn Gilmar's private force, were swiftly dealt with—they would be tried and executed for treason after the dust settled from tonight's coup.

But it seemed like their plan had had a flaw in it: Adriana should have been on that sled with the queen, but Steven's face was grim as he maneuvered to land on the roof.

Taron launched himself at the human, knocking him from the sled and onto the icy ground. "Where is she?" he roared, punching the idiot who'd left her at the palace.

"She couldn't board," the soldier shouted, fighting to throw Taron off.

His moves would have been decent if he were a Rendian, but his strength was nothing compared to Taron's. He lifted the man's shoulders and slammed him back down so his head bounced on the tiled roof.

"How could you leave her?"

Then strong hands closed on his shoulders, tugging him back. "Taron, wait!" Zeema's voice—he hadn't heard her speak in weeks, it seemed, and then only in timid whispers because the regent had always been near.

"Stop it, you're killing him."

Taron growled but released the human. Steven fell back with a groan and didn't move. Maybe Taron broke his neck. He couldn't find it in himself to feel remorse.

"Explain," he commanded, fixing his younger cousin with a glare. He didn't care that she was his monarch at that moment. He'd done everything in his power to save her, yes, but if Adriana was left behind...

"She told us to leave," Zeema whispered. She hugged herself and added, "She helped me, and then she didn't have the time to climb out. If she'd tried, the soldiers could have shot Steven or me through the window. But she told us to go."

Her big blue eyes were so earnest and frightened, Taron knew she was telling the truth. Adriana *would* have done exactly that. She'd taken care of others, made sure the queen was safe, and sacrificed herself.

"*Fuck!*" he roared, uncaring of who might hear them.

"What will you do?" Zeema asked, her voice tremulous.

Next to them, Steven groaned and got to his feet.

The queen rushed over to him and peered into his eyes. "Are you all right?"

The man nodded, then straightened and faced Taron. "I'm sorry. But our mission objective was to save Queen Zeema and disable her collar. We've done that. Adriana knew what she was doing, and she ordered me to leave."

Taron closed his eyes. The feeling of unease that blossomed in his chest every time he was apart from her now gaped inside him, a black hole of rage and despair. His Adriana could be dead already or caught by the regent. What if he'd collared her?

"I need to return," he murmured. He lifted his head and looked at the queen. "I need to help her."

She nodded. "Go."

"I thought I'd be the one to lead you to safety," he said, placing a hand on her shoulder. "We'd agreed..." He shook his head. "But I can't leave her."

Steven cleared his throat from beside him. "Sir, I'll escort her."

Taron resisted the urge to roll his eyes. "Much good you'll be." But he sighed, took one of the spears from the hover sled, and threw it to Zeema. "Take this. Stun anyone who would dare stand in your path."

She nodded, then inclined her head to the human. "Let's go."

They disappeared over the edge of the roof, leaving Taron alone beneath the clear, diamond-studded sky.

He didn't have the time to admire the universe, though.

He jumped onto the hover sled and turned it back toward the shining black palace.

He had a woman to save and an enemy to kill.

23

Adriana

"REGENT YAROH AD Gilmar murdered the king and most of his Cabinet..."

Kol's voice reverberated around the room, which was otherwise completely silent. The guests all stood, no longer reclining on the divans, no longer sipping wine or crunching on fried vissnae. Their faces were illuminated by the light coming from a large screen that had flickered to life on the broad chamber wall.

Adriana limped into the room. The guards didn't even notice, so busy were they staring at the live transmission of the two Naals brothers.

Kol stood in front of a regiment of soldiers, Lhett a step behind him. They both looked splendid in their full armor and clearly held the soldiers' attention.

"The queen has been successfully rescued from the

palace just half an hour ago. She is being escorted to a safe location until her collar can be removed."

The small green delegates chittered loudly, their voices translated by Adriana's ear implant. They were *not* happy with this revelation.

"Shut it down!" The regent stormed ahead, pointing at a servant standing by the wall. "Kill it, now."

The servant scrambled to obey, but the damage was done. As one, every single person in the room turned to look at the regent.

"These men," Gilmar spat, "are nothing more than disgraced soldiers who would stop at nothing to take the power. *They* are the ones who killed the king, and if I hadn't protected the queen, they would have murdered her, too. Did you know that Lhett ad Naals is the next in line for the throne?"

Hanne gasped at that; Adriana guessed that the former general hadn't mentioned that to his human charge. Then Hanne's gaze fell on her, and she broke away from the table, running to help.

Adriana swayed with relief. Maybe she could just lie down for a moment...

A guard rushed forward and put out his spear to prevent Hanne from reaching Adriana. He didn't fire at her, but the movement was clear and menacing: make another move, and you'll get hurt.

Mika appeared behind Hanne and pulled her back, her dark eyes narrowed.

Then Jean was there, pushing them both behind him. "Where is the queen, then?" he called out.

"Yes, yes, show us the queen," the green-skinned delegates screeched, their tentacles now waving in a wholly different pattern.

The regent hesitated for a single second. Then he drew back his shoulders and plastered on a smile. "She has been taken to a safe location by her guards. This criminal," he calmly continued and pointed at Adriana, "tried to ambush her in the bathroom."

Two more guards appeared by Adriana's sides, and they hoisted her up by her arms, their grips painfully hard. She struggled, but she was so tired, and everything hurt.

"That's not true!" Mika shouted, throwing herself against Jean's hold. "Look at her! Look what they did!"

"The queen is wearing a tracking device," the regent continued without a blink. "She was never in any real danger, thanks to the brave sacrifices of my men." He spread his hands in a conciliatory gesture. "Come, I don't want this incident to destroy our lovely evening. Drinks, anyone?"

The members of the human delegation who hadn't been in on the plan stared at Adriana as though wondering whether she really had tried to murder the queen.

"He's lying," she tried to yell, but her voice was too hoarse from the regent's choking. "The queen is with Steven!"

Jean motioned to Ben to grab Mika, who would have impaled herself on the guard's spear—she was still shouting with rage. Hanne was quietly moving back, looking at the window, possibly planning an escape. Then Jean jumped forward, slapped the spear aside, and tackled the guard. A commotion rose, chairs overturned as the Rendian nobles retreated and the soldiers advanced.

Then Jean twitched violently and collapsed on the floor; a second guard had shocked him with a bolt of electricity, and now the big Canadian lay there, his eyes rolled back.

Mika stopped struggling against Ben, her hands flying to

her mouth, and the doctor tried to check Jean's vitals. The guards wouldn't let him.

Adriana shouted at the other humans to help, but they stood huddled in a group, apart from Grahame, who was watching the chaos unfold from a corner, his arms crossed over his chest. He wouldn't step in to help until it was clear which side would win, she knew, and at the moment, the regent certainly seemed in control.

As though he could hear her thoughts, Gilmar motioned to the musicians who still stood on a raised dais at the other end of the room. "A song, please," he demanded, "to put us in a better mood after this, ah, inconvenience."

Adriana's guards held her tight, not giving an inch, no matter how she struggled.

"When the people find out what you did at Murrun, they'll revolt," she yelled, her hair flying everywhere. She likely looked deranged if the delegates' shocked glances were any indication. They didn't know her, didn't know humans, but they did know Gilmar and had been doing business with Rendians for decades. *Of course* they were more likely to believe him if it was just her word against his. He could spin the tale however he wanted—and there was a dead guard in the bathroom to prove she'd been a part of the attack. The other, younger guard, would also wake up soon and testify that she'd stabbed him in the neck to tranquilize him.

"Guards, please take the distressed lady to a holding cell. I'll deal with her later." He pointed at Jean's prone form. "And take that gentleman to the infirmary, please."

Adriana couldn't believe her ears. The man knew the queen was gone, yet he was acting as though this was just a minor blip in his plan. He was either mad or had an ace up his sleeve that they didn't know about—and tracking

Zeema's collar wasn't one of them. The resin would have taken care of that.

"Don't listen to him," she screamed as the guards turned her toward the door. "Listen to the Naals brothers!"

"Silence her," the regent commanded, his voice no longer jovial.

A painful jolt shocked Adriana's body for the second time that week, and then everything went black.

24

Taron

WITH ANGER and fear churning in his stomach, he jumped on the hover sled and sped back to the palace. He needed to find Adriana and make sure she was still alive first. Then he would bundle her up and carry her to the safe house where the queen and Steven were hopefully resting at that very moment. And he would never let her go.

This plan was too risky, he'd known it from the start, and he'd sacrificed Adriana's safety for Zeema's. It was the most difficult decision he'd ever had to make.

Adriana would have gone through with the plan with your blessing or without it. The truth rang clearly inside his mind. His human was brave and stubborn, and once she'd learned of their political trouble, she'd been focused on helping them.

Now she might die because of her generosity.

He neared the sheer palace wall, counting the windows

from the ground up to find the ones in the great reception hall. It was situated in one of the large claw-like towers and offered spectacular views over the city and the frozen plains beyond. The large windows were a luxury only the kings and queens of Rendu could afford—a show of wealth, because preserving what little heat they had was the main concern for most of his people.

The hover sled allowed him to approach the windows from below. He had no intention of giving away his position. He was vulnerable enough, exposed on the sled without the protective shell of an airship around him, but he couldn't afford to waste the time it would take to get another aircraft. He needed to see what was going on in the hall.

Rising ever so slowly, he poked his head above the windowsill. The first thing he noticed was that the large screen had been turned off—it should have been playing Kol's message on a loop.

The city below him was already roiling. Every Rendian with access to a broadcasting device had already seen the video, because they'd sent it through the emergency line, which usually served to inform the nation of military drills or upcoming quakes and thermal eruptions.

The people were not pleased with what they heard, and if the regent didn't surrender peacefully, he'd have a furious mob hammering down the palace doors within the hour.

But Gilmar didn't seem to be worried. In fact, he stood at the head of the table, grinning broadly, and lifted his glass in a toast. Taron couldn't hear his words through the multi-paned window, but something definitely didn't fit...

At that moment, Taron glimpsed two guards carrying a red-clothed bundle out of the reception hall.

Adriana.

His body went cold with fury and purpose. He quickly

measured the window with his gaze—if he tried opening it from the outside, the guards would strike him down, and the hover sled would crash on the streets below...

The hover sled.

Taron looked at the control panel in front of him, then appraised the sled's pointed nose. It was made of the same titanium alloy as the armor the Rendian soldiers wore, light but hard and durable. With enough speed...

He glanced back up, calculating. If he crashed— He stamped down on the thought, flicked a switch, and reversed the sled away from the palace wall. He couldn't afford for doubts to creep in. There was no time: if he tried fighting his way through the palace corridors, only the ancestors knew how long it would take him to reach Adriana. His face was probably plastered on every guardsman's tablet, and until the regent's private force was dismantled, every soldier had the potential for being an enemy. He wouldn't even know who to fight.

At the distance of fifty feet, he stopped, assessing. If he hit too low or too high, the obsidian wall would shear off either the bottom of the sled or his head. The vehicle would be a ruin anyway, but he thought his head might be worth protecting. Even if it was currently spewing all sorts of warnings at him.

But his heart beat for one woman only, and she was in there, injured, maybe dead. He needed to get to her, and this was the fastest way to do it.

He hit a button on his wrist cuff to activate his full armor. It covered his head, molding around his neck and jaw. Then he typed the trajectory into the sled's autopilot system and took up the stolen spear. It held enough charge for five stuns—or three kills. Taron kept it set for stunning, because dispatching as many guards as possible would take precedence over killing them. After that, he'd have to stab and fight them in close combat.

Shit. His brothers would tell him he was being an idiot. But he thought that deep down, they might understand. They weren't as immune to their human protégées as they pretended.

With a deep breath, Taron hit the ignition button, then threw himself on the floor of the sled. The vehicle accelerated to full speed in under three seconds, hurtling toward the palace wall.

Taron kept his head down, praying he'd calculated the distance correctly. In another breath, he could be nothing but a bloody splatter on the black obsidian wall...

Crash.

Glass flew, shattering around him, and Taron threw his arms up to shield his face from the shards. They landed on his back, his legs, but didn't hurt him; the armor did its job of protecting him.

Shrieks followed, yelps of terror and surprise, and then his hover sled crashed against the far wall of the chamber. He was thrown clear and flew, but rolled at the last moment to break his fall.

Taron crouched, spear still clutched in his hand. A quick mental check told him he hadn't broken any bones. Then he surveyed the scene around him.

Most of the human delegation appeared unharmed; they'd been squished in a corner before he landed, so they were out of the shards' way. But the big engineer lay on the floor, a large splinter of glass stuck in his thigh.

"Shit!" the human doctor yelled from next to him. "Are you insane?"

His shout broke the spell of silence in the room. Two Rendian noblewomen shrieked, jumping up and escaping out of the room. Taron let them go, even though he noted who they were and would make sure they suffered for having allied themselves with Gilmar.

Mika hollered, "Get the fucker!"

Taron would have grinned, but that would have taken his focus away from the regent.

The man deposited his goblet and activated his armor with a sigh. "Oh, Taron," he said. "Such a waste. Your little plaything is dead, and now you'll join her. Then I'll find your idiot brothers and make sure they never trouble me again." He snapped his fingers. "Guards."

What incited Taron's rage the most was the bored cadence of Gilmar's voice. As though none of them were important enough to get riled up about. He'd said that Adriana was dead...

No. He couldn't let himself be distracted. His objective was to reach her first. One step at a time.

He didn't dare turn his back on Gilmar—a mistake like that would cost him his life. The guards were advancing on him, their gazes wary but hard. He didn't want to kill them, but with time running short...

He attacked, putting his back to the wall so the guards had little space to move. They got in each others' way, which told him they weren't used to fighting together. He mowed one down with a vicious blow of his spear and rammed the butt of the weapon into the man's face. The sickening crunch reverberated down his arm, but he didn't stop. The next guardsman landed a glancing blow to his leg; he was lucky his armor was activated, or he might have lost a kneecap.

The guards' faces and weapons blended into a blur, and he became a machine, his mind blank and his every strike deadly. The two men left standing exchanged wary glances

—they had their orders and would kill him, but they'd seen him bludgeon five of their colleagues.

What they didn't know was that Taron's weapon had lost its charge. He could pick up any of the fallen soldiers' weapons, but it would cost him...

"No!" Hanne's yell splintered his attention.

She and Mika were standing over Adriana, guarding her lifeless body on the floor. Now the regent stood in front of them, a menacing figure a head taller than either of them. He pushed Hanne out of the way, took Mika by the collar, and flung her onto a table by the wall. The tiny human scientist landed with a crash and collapsed.

Then Gilmar grabbed Adriana.

Taron's thoughts blanked. His limbs moved on pure instinct, some ingrained reflexes guiding him until he dispatched one guard with a stab to his throat, the blow so powerful it pierced the armor. He took hold of the other and broke his neck like a twig.

"Stop," the regent shouted. "Stop or she dies."

He had Adriana in a choke hold, his armored hand around her slender throat.

Taron blinked, returning to himself. If he gave the regent time to act, the asshole would crush Adriana's windpipe. She was alive, that much was certain, her eyelids fluttering. Something cracked open in Taron's chest. She was *alive* and breathing, yet caught. He would do anything to save her.

"Drop your weapon," Gilmar commanded. "Now."

The spear clattered to the floor, useless. He couldn't risk throwing it at the regent as he'd intended—the man was fast and could turn Adriana into the spear's trajectory.

From somewhere behind him, Taron registered the panicked chittering of the trade delegates. One of them was clearly trying to communicate with their spaceship in orbit, but this fight would be over long before any reinforcements arrived, either from the little green men or Taron's own brothers.

"Let her go," he growled at the regent. "This isn't her fight."

Gilmar shook Adriana without looking at her. "Yes, but she made it her fight the moment she helped that bitch escape. I've had to listen to her whining for *weeks*, and now she's gone?"

Adriana blinked again but remained limp in the regent's grip. Taron met her gaze for the briefest second, then focused his attention back at her captor.

"Think of what you're doing," Taron said. "The delegates—"

"Fuck the delegates," the regent spat. "I've been working on bringing this forsaken planet out of this rut, to establish new trade routes, and bring in more money. All at the cost of a couple of villages' worth of fucking peasants who wouldn't know their own shit from platinum. Do you have any idea how rich the ore is in those mines?"

He was breathing hard, gripping Adriana. Her face was turning red—surely that couldn't be good. From the corner of his eye, Taron saw the human doctor creep closer to Mika, who now stirred on the floor. Hanne was crouched beside her, pressing a napkin to a gash on her friend's forehead.

Adriana's eyes glittered, though, and her hand inched slowly upward. Did she have a plan?

"You can't think the nation will accept you as their ruler," Taron said to stall Gilmar. "Even if the queen disappeared, you'd have to wait for a year to have her declared dead. And then Lhett is the next in line."

Clearly, the regent didn't hear the shouting from the streets. It was nothing more than a distant hum, but Taron expected the protests would grow in number before morning. Gilmar would have nowhere to run.

"I'll find her and then I won't have to wait for a year to have her declared dead. I'll kill all of you." The regent's voice grew cold, and he squeezed Adriana tighter. She gasped. "Starting with her."

At that moment, Adriana reached inside the front of her dress and swung her arm up. The movement was too fast for Taron to see what she did, but Gilmar howled and dropped her to the floor.

Blood gushed from behind his hands, and his screams echoed from the vaulted ceiling.

Adriana knelt on the floor, gasping for breath, and the regent's boots caught her in the side as he flailed and kicked around.

Taron leaped forward, whisking her to safety. Then they both stared down at Gilmar, whose hands fell away— and Taron saw that one of the wooden sticks she'd used to pin up her hair was lodged in his eye.

The man pulled it out, pressed the heel of his palm to his eye, and rolled to his feet.

"How is he still standing?" Adriana whispered, her voice cracked and barely audible.

Taron drew her farther back, wary of what Gilmar might do. He picked up a spear from one of the soldiers. The rest of the people in the chamber remained motionless: the three delegates armed themselves with short clubs and were glaring at everyone, the humans stood rooted to the spot in the corner, and the Rendian nobles who hadn't escaped wore matching masks of disinterest. They wouldn't help the regent, who was clearly losing.

He walked to stand in front of Gilmar. "Will you surrender honorably and stand trial for your crimes?" he asked.

Gilmar spat in his face.

Taron sighed and wiped the spit off with his palm. "The outcome will be the same for you, but your family might—" He ducked a blow the regent aimed at him. "Think, man. If you keep—"

Again, he evaded a punch. Gilmar's hits were slowing. He would likely go into shock soon. The wound wasn't fatal. He would lose an eye, but that would only matter until Queen Zeema held a trial for him. Taron had no doubt that she would sentence her tormentor to death.

The regent plucked a small dagger from his belt and launched himself at Taron.

It was time to end this.

With a swipe of his spear, Taron knocked the disgraced man onto his back. He caught the flash of surprise in his eyes the second before he flicked the weapon's setting to killing force and slammed the point into the regent's chest.

Gilmar twitched once, then went still.

The room around him erupted in noise, some of the humans escaped, and a guard groaned feebly on the floor. But Taron only saw Adriana.

She leaned on the table, her dress and hair disheveled, her throat and cheek already bruising purple. But she was looking at him.

He stepped forward and knelt in front of her. With a flick of his fingers, he deactivated his armor's helmet and hung his head.

"I'm sorry you had to see that. I'm sorry I didn't arrive sooner."

His human dropped to her knees and hugged him. Her

warm, soft arms wrapped around his shoulders, and her head came to rest against his chest.

"I'm so glad you're alive," she mumbled. "I was so worried."

He held her close for a moment, until she gasped. He gently pried her away from him to check her injuries. "Woman, you're crazy. I don't have a scratch on me, and still you worry?"

He touched the bruise blooming around her eye, carefully, but she flinched in pain anyway.

"Who did this to you?" he growled.

Adriana shook her head. "It doesn't matter. He's dead."

"Did you...?"

"No. Zeema killed him. He'd been torturing her, so she cut off his hand and stabbed him."

Taron raised his eyebrows. "Good."

Adriana nodded, but her eyes were wide, her pupils dilated so much the brown irises were barely visible. "Yeah. And I, um, stabbed the regent," she added.

Taron took hold of her shoulders and peered at her. "Are you all right?"

"Mm-hm."

She swayed and would have toppled over if he weren't supporting her.

Taron turned to where the human doctor was tending to Jean's injuries. "Help me," he called. "She's..."

Adriana passed out. Taron cradled her in his arms, swiping her hair away from her face. Then Ben was at his side, checking her pulse.

"We'll take her to my suite," he declared. "I'll need to do some x-rays to see if anything's broken."

He went as if to take her from Taron's arms. Taron

snarled at him, and the human lifted his hands up in surrender.

"Fine, you bring her. Do you think you could have someone help carry Jean as well? He's a big guy."

Taron faced a Rendian man standing by the wall. He was clearly uncomfortable and trying to sneak out of the room, but Taron pinned him with a glare.

"Carry the engineer."

"Do you have any idea who I..." the nobleman began, but Taron cut him off.

"You'll be dead if you don't help." He had very little patience for these traitors, and he was certain Zeema would strip them of their titles for supporting Gilmar.

The man grabbed Jean, though, and motioned for two of his friends to come help as well. Together, they formed a procession that wound its way through the palace halls toward the humans' quarters. The uninjured members of their crew shut themselves into their own rooms, their gazes frightened.

Taron suspected they might petition for a ship to return to Earth sooner than planned, but that was a worry for tomorrow.

Tonight, he needed to care for his Adriana.

Ben assumed command the moment they entered his medical suite. Jean was deposited on one bed, Mika on another, and Taron laid Adriana down on a stretcher by the wall. The human doctor put on a white coat and washed his hands, then told Taron to wait outside.

"No. I can help."

Ben sighed. "Ugh, fine. But only do what I tell you to do. And scrub your hands with that soap first. Twice."

Taron stepped to the door of the suite long enough to call a friendly guard, whom he sent out to find Lieutenant

Anilla and Kol. Hanne was sitting at Mika's bed, holding her friend's hand, but retreated to the corner when Ben approached Mika with a needle.

"I don't do well with, um, that," she stammered, pointing at the doctor's hand.

"You don't have to watch," Ben told her in a surprisingly kind voice. "Go wash that blood off you, and I'll send someone for you when it's done."

The astrophysicist fled the suite, the door sliding shut behind her. Now Taron and Ben remained alone with the three unconscious humans.

"I'll stitch Mika's wound up first to stop the bleeding," the doctor informed Taron. "Then I'll take their x-rays and maybe an ultrasound to make sure no one is bleeding internally."

Taron glanced down at Adriana's limp form. "What can I do?"

"Get some ice for her bruises. She's breathing well, so her windpipe probably isn't too badly injured, and her lungs are okay, but I want to check her as soon as possible. She might have broken ribs."

Taron nodded and found an ice pack in Ben's refrigerator. It didn't escape him that his planet was frozen solid, yet he was cooling Adriana's cheek and neck with an Earth-made pouch filled with a blue gel. He swiped back her hair from her forehead and tried to quell his worry. Her breaths remained steady, her heartbeat strong.

"Wake up," he whispered. "Please."

"Can you pass me the bandages?" Ben asked.

Taron sighed and positioned the ice pack so it was pressed against Adriana's cheek, then went to help the doctor. Together, they worked on Mika's forehead, then Jean's leg, where a long, deep gash was still pulsing out blood. Ben pinched his lips into a tight line at the sight, and they performed a minor surgery to repair a nicked vein. Some very creative cursing was involved in the procedure.

Then it was Adriana's turn: her ribs proved to be cracked, not broken, and her head injuries were just bruises.

"We'll see how it goes when she wakes up," Ben told him. "But don't worry too much. I think she's sleeping now."

He filled a syringe with a clear liquid and injected it into the bag of water hanging above Adriana. A thin clear tube led down to her arm; the doctor had explained how it worked, and Taron had shuddered at the thought of having something like that attached to himself. But he deferred to Ben's judgment when it came to Adriana's health.

This was a serious problem he hadn't considered before.

He glanced at Ben, who was now putting ointment on Jean's burn, the spot where the guard had struck him with the electric spear.

"Would you be willing to stay here?" he asked. "If...if she does."

The doctor looked up, surprise written all over his face. "I didn't think you'd let me. Not after..." He waved a hand toward the refrigerator. "You know, the blood."

Taron grimaced. "I'm not saying I like it. But...if she decides to stay, she'd need someone to take care of her. In a way I can't, I mean."

It hurt his pride to admit it. But human bodies were so fragile—and just different enough from Rendians that their doctors wouldn't know what to do with them. They might even hurt Adriana if they tried treating her. And if she ever wanted to have a child... He couldn't even fathom what that would mean for her.

"I could stay," Ben said, his expression pensive. "But..." The gleam in his eyes turned calculating.

Taron frowned. "What would you want in return?"

"A chance to study Rendians."

He couldn't help it: a low growl escaped him. But the doctor didn't seem scared. He shrugged and went back to nursing Jean.

Taron thought about it. "You can study *me* in exchange for teaching me your art."

"You would do that?" Ben's eyebrows went up.

"I'd do anything for her. But you must keep your research...within reason."

The human chuckled. "I won't cut you up if that's what you're afraid of. But I want to know how your body works, what your chemical composition is, how strong you are. Mostly noninvasive stuff."

"Mostly?"

"I won't do anything to hurt you, trust me."

"Hm." Taron didn't trust the doctor, but unless they imported another human on Rendu and convinced them to stay, he was Adriana's best option. "Fine."

"It might take years to teach you all I know," Ben remarked while he taped a large white bandage over Jean's burn.

"Fine," Taron repeated. He wanted Ben gone so he could keep vigil over Adriana in peace.

"You'd do that for her?"

Taron glanced up. The doctor's question was earnest, without a hint of judgment. If anything, he seemed sad. Wistful.

So he answered with the full truth. "I'd do anything."

25

Adriana

AW, man, I should really stop passing out.

Adriana's first thought was that she'd spent a month on Rendu and had been knocked unconscious more often than in her entire life before that. It spoke to the fact that she was insane for even thinking about staying here, but her resolution hadn't wavered. Taron was stuck with her whether he liked it or not.

Taron.

She struggled to sit up. She needed to find him and thank him for saving her—

"Aah!" A yelp escaped her lips. Her entire chest hurt like a bitch, and she slumped back on the pillow, clutching her side.

"Adriana! What's wrong?"

Taron's beautiful face appeared over her, pale and drawn with worry.

"Where does it hurt?"

She grimaced. Now that her body was waking up properly, it *all* hurt. But she had a sneaking suspicion that Taron would freak if she told him the whole truth, so she said, "My ribs, a little."

"They're cracked," Ben announced and stepped into her field of vision. "Give me a sec to check her over, Naals, then I'll leave you two for a bit."

Adriana glanced around. She only now realized they were in Ben's medical suite, with two other beds occupied. On one lay Jean, his eyes still closed, but his chest rose and fell with deep, restful breaths. On the other lay Mika *and* Kol, both passed out cold.

"Is she—" Adriana began, then added, "Was he hurt as well?"

"No," Ben replied while he shone a light into her eyes. "But he was raging around, so I poked him with a small dose of epinephrine. I think it's already worn off, but he's still sleeping."

Adriana looked at Taron and raised her eyebrows.

He nodded in confirmation. "Mika will be fine, she just lost some blood, and we haven't had the time to change her stained clothes, so Kol saw her all bloodied up and went...a little crazy."

He rubbed his jaw then, and Adriana thought she saw a pale bruise there.

"Did he punch you?" She stroked his skin, so smooth and cool.

Her alien shrugged. "Eh, it's nothing. I'm more worried about you."

She held his gaze while Ben gently pressed on her ribs and listened to her lungs.

Finally, the Dutch doctor removed his stethoscope and

grinned. "You'll be just fine. Now I'll go grab some food. I'll be back in fifteen minutes." He pointed at Taron. "She needs *rest*, is that clear?"

To Adriana's surprise, Taron nodded. "Got it."

Adriana didn't wait for the door to close behind Ben. She wrapped her arms around Taron's neck and pulled him down, using his surprise to press a hard kiss on his lips.

He grumbled but kissed her back, his blue eyes drifting closed. His hand came to cup her cheek, and it felt amazing.

She giggled against his lips. "I can use you as my personal ice pack," she joked. "Though you're not really portable, so that's a downside."

A serious frown replaced his smile. "I thought you were dead," he said. "When I crashed through the window and saw you lying on the floor..."

"Wait." Adriana pressed her palm over his mouth. "You crashed through a *window*?" She craned her neck to check him over, but he didn't seem to be injured. "Are you okay?"

Taron gingerly eased himself onto the stretcher next to her, and she let him wrap her in a careful embrace. "Well, I didn't just accidentally crash," he told her. "I drove the hover sled right into the chamber."

She squeezed her eyes shut in horror. "You could have been killed."

"So could you."

She opened her eyes and found him looking at her, his expression fierce.

"In that moment, nothing else mattered."

She sensed his frustration that he couldn't prevent her from getting injured, so she stroked his hair, his brow, until he gradually relaxed under her touch. "I'm okay now."

He let out a great sigh. "Just don't expect me to let you out of my sight anytime soon."

With a smile, she replied, "Well, lucky for you that I'm staying here, then."

He stilled, his entire big body going rigid. His voice was gravelly when he spoke. "So you...didn't change your mind?"

Adriana shook her head.

"And you'll stay with *me*?"

Silly alien. "Who else? I love *you*, remember?"

He groaned and buried his face in her neck. Adriana hissed in pain. The bruises Gilmar had given her were very tender despite the painkillers Ben pumped into her system.

Taron immediately jerked back—and tumbled off the stretcher.

A round of cursing told her he was fine, and she giggled. When he reappeared by her side, he apologized for causing her pain.

"I wish I could kill him all over again," he admitted. "Once was not enough."

She smiled sadly at him. "I wish you didn't have to kill any more people."

He drew back. "Did you not want me to?"

His frown was fierce, but Adriana sensed more uncertainty than anger beneath it. Despite the pain, she struggled to sit up.

"Taron, I'm grateful you saved me. You saved us all—the queen, me, your people. Probably the entire human delegation. Who knows what would have happened if Gilmar had had his way." She extended her hand and waited until he entwined his fingers with hers. "He was a horrible man, and I'm not sorry he's gone. The same goes for the soldiers who willingly followed him. They *hurt the queen*, Taron."

The memory from the bathroom had anger spiking

inside her. That guard got what he deserved. So did the regent.

"Thank you for understanding," Taron murmured. He leaned his forehead against hers, then kissed her, his cool tongue stroking hers, until she was panting and clinging on to him.

Adriana wished she could return to her room and have her way with him, but she suspected her bruised ribs would protest. She broke off the kiss and glanced at the other sleeping people in the room.

"They'll be fine, right?" she asked.

Taron nodded. "So says the doctor."

"And the queen?"

He sighed. "I had to leave her with your human, Steven, even though I wanted to kill him for leaving you at the palace." He held up a hand when she started to protest. "I know, you told him to go. I'm still not happy with him. But he escorted Zeema to the safe house where Lhett joined them a little while ago. They took off her collar with the key Gilmar carried."

Adriana sighed with relief. The young queen was safe, and their mission was successful. "And the rest of the guards?"

"They surrendered—they saw the broadcast and immediately threw down their weapons. I think they realized the people would have torn them to pieces if they'd resisted. They'll be tried for treason after the dust settles."

This was all great. But she still wasn't entirely convinced. "How about the villagers? The ones stuck inside the mines?"

Taron chuckled. "You don't have to worry about *everyone*, you know? But a regiment of soldiers has been sent to the area to help close down the mines again, to seal them, and return the villagers safely to their homes."

Adriana melted back against the pillow. "Oof. That's okay, then." Tiredness washed over her in a wave, and she closed her eyes.

Cold lips pressed to her forehead. "Rest now. I'll stay with you."

She searched blindly for his hand and then squeezed his fingers hard. "Thank you," she murmured, just before she drifted back to sleep.

26

Adriana

BEN INSISTED on keeping her in the medical suite for another two days.

"You can't do anything strenuous anyway, and here, you'll have company, at least," he told her, indicating Mika's and Jean's beds.

They were both recovering well, though Mika's head was still wrapped in bandages, and Jean couldn't put any weight on his leg. The Canadian engineer also snored like a chainsaw, a fact which Lieutenant Anilla, who visited him daily, found 'charming.' Adriana and Mika had exchanged a loaded glance at that and asked Ben to provide some ear plugs.

Taron joined them for all meal times, bringing Rendian delicacies to Adriana. She thought it was a courting ritual of sorts and ate whatever he brought—she even choked down some of the slimy, cold jelly of dubious origin while Mika laughed her ass off in the next bed.

More interesting still, Kol kept inventing reasons to drop by the medical suite. Ben had banned him from bringing his pet horeen into the room; the large, tame beast had been kept captive by the regent, who had known exactly where to strike to hurt the Naals brothers the most. Now the scarlet fox-like creature would sit in front of the door, yipping loudly until Kol left with her again.

Mika blushed furiously every time he arrived and refused to talk to anyone about it. Adriana confided in her friends and told them she would not be leaving Rendu with them when the time came for humans to return to Earth. She hadn't yet asked for official permission from the queen, but she didn't think her request would be denied.

Her friends weren't all that surprised by her decision.

"He can still fly you home later if you ever decide to return," Mika said, ever practical.

Hanne's smile was surprisingly wicked as she added, "I'm not sure he'd let her go, though. Judging by the look he gave her just before..."

Adriana's cheeks flooded with warmth. Ben promised her she could leave the medical suite that afternoon, and Taron kissed her hard and left with a promise of a surprise.

She couldn't wait to see what he had in mind.

If she had any say in it, they would be naked while he presented her with whatever it was.

Her heart hurt at the thought of her two best friends leaving. She would have to create new bonds with Rendians, meet her new neighbors and perhaps Taron's extended family. She wished she could get to know the queen better as well—the young woman surprised her with her strength and resolve.

The door of the medical suite slid open, revealing Taron's tall form. He was dressed in plain clothes and so handsome, she got a gut-punch feeling every time she looked at him. What did she ever do to deserve such a man?

But he was staring at her with the same intensity. She trembled under the weight of his gaze. Taron crossed over to her in three long strides and completely ignored the other people. With great care, he helped her put on Rendian winter gear: the soft leather pants, the thick wool coat and hat. She laced up her boots, then climbed from the stretcher.

"Thanks for everything, Ben," she said, nodding at the doctor. "I'll be back for—eek!"

Her words were cut off as Taron lifted her.

"What are you doing?" she squeaked. She grabbed on to him to keep from tipping over but relaxed a moment later.

He held her tight and seemed completely relaxed. He would not let her fall.

"I'm taking you home." His deep voice rumbled against her.

Adriana craned her neck, glancing back in time to see Mika and Hanne's curious faces poking around the medical suite door. They both gave her thumbs-up and disappeared.

Hmph. So much for good friends—they let her be kidnapped by this alien without so much as a protest.

With a smile, she pressed a kiss to the underside of Taron's jaw. "Hey, um, my room is that way." She pointed in the other direction.

He groaned. "I know. And believe me, I want to carry you there and take you up against the wall. But I have something better planned."

Out they went, into the cold evening. Wind blew fiercely through the snowy city streets, sharpened by the narrow passages between buildings. They passed the entrance to the large marketplace, walked down an avenue lined with shops, and rounded a corner by the school.

A large white building came into view, and Adriana wondered who lived—or worked—there. It was a three-story mansion that seemed to be hewn all from one giant piece of blue-tinged rock: it glittered like ice in the last rays of the feeble winter sun.

Taron came to a stop in front of it. He shifted her weight around and raised his wrist cuff to the tall double doors.

"What is this place?" Adriana asked quietly as he carried her into the spacious entrance hall. Her murmur echoed around the chamber. The doors closed behind them, operated by some hidden mechanism, and the room immediately lost some of its chill.

"It's our home," Taron replied. He took the stairs on the left two at a time, his long legs eating the distance without effort. "We'll live in this wing."

Adriana blinked. "What?"

They walked past several open doors now and met a number of Rendians who were busy tidying up.

"This is my family's house," Taron explained. "When our parents died, Kol took over the family business while Lhett and I joined the army. But we all have apartments here. Ours will be in this wing."

Gaping, Adriana stared around her. *Palace* was a better description for the building. *House* simply didn't do it justice.

"Your room is in here?" She craned her neck and tried to peek through one of the doors they passed, but Taron's stride was too fast.

"*Rooms*," he corrected her. "This entire wing is ours."

A *wing*. He had a whole wing of this enormous place.

"Um. I guess that'll have to do," she joked.

He growled quietly and picked up his pace.

They reached the door at the very end of the corridor. Two men were moving around, dusting and putting the final touches on the room.

"Out, now." Taron's gravelly voice brooked no argument. "Clear the floor."

The men nodded and left without a word, closing the door behind them.

It was then that Adriana noticed an enormous bed that dominated the space. Taron set her down gently, still careful of her injuries. Though she'd improved over the past couple of days, her ribs were still very tender, while her face and neck were mottled with bruises.

But Taron didn't seem to mind.

He took her face in his big palms and kissed her, gentle at first, but Adriana needed more. She rose to her knees and held on to him, opening her mouth and allowing him to plunder.

"I don't want to hurt you," Taron groaned as she dug her hands under his coat and shirt to find the smooth, hard planes of his abs.

Adriana hummed against his lips. "Do you trust me?" she asked.

He dropped his forehead to her shoulder and let her undo the laces of his coat. "Yes."

"Then believe me when I tell you that I want this."

She peeled the clothes off him, one by one, until he stood in front of her in his pants, laces already undone. He was magnificent, his skin flushed a pale blue, his every muscle defined. The shoulder spikes added a rough edge to his physique.

"You're so—" she began but stopped the moment her gaze met his.

He was looking at her with such intensity, her thoughts stuttered to a stop, but her heart picked up its pace, thudding against her ribs.

"Taron?"

He stepped forward and silently, gently undressed her, his white eyebrows drawn down as though this was a task that required his full attention. Her coat, sweater, and pants were discarded on the floor, followed by her socks and t-shirt.

"This vision haunts me in my dreams," her alien warrior murmured.

She knelt on the bed before him, dressed only in her underwear—a plain black bra and panties, chosen for their practicality back on Earth, when she didn't even know that Taron ad Naals would steal her heart.

She might have to visit Vinsha in her amazing shop again and see if she could get some more...elaborate lingerie here. Taron would surely appreciate some lace.

He ran his palms lightly over her, barely skimming her skin, but even that fleeting touch raised goosebumps all over her torso. Her nipples hardened into points, begging for his attention.

"Take it off," she whispered as he hooked a finger under her bra strap and caressed her collarbone with one rough pad.

But Taron shook his head. "Not yet."

He lay her back on the soft pillows and lowered himself over her, keeping his weight on his forearms. With kiss after kiss, he drove her wild—without ever taking off her underwear. His cold lips traced a path from the hollow of her throat, between her breasts, down to her navel, yet he refused to touch her where she most needed him.

Adriana burned for him. Her skin grew damp with perspiration, and she let her hands roam all over him—but he wouldn't allow her to take off his pants.

"Taron, please," she begged. "I need...*ohhh*."

His mouth closed on her sensitive nipple, and he stroked her over the thin cotton. She was *so close*, so damn close... Adriana sneaked one hand down to her panties. One flick, maybe two, over her clit, and she'd go off—

Taron grabbed her hand and pinned it on the bed beside her hip. Then he caught the other one and held her there, effortlessly, while he continued his slow sensual assault. Hours passed, or maybe just minutes, but Adriana's entire world narrowed down to the feeling of his lips on her skin. His tongue drew erotic patterns over her heated body, always stopping just an inch shy of where she ached the most.

She thrashed beneath him and finally hooked her legs around his waist for leverage. Before Taron realized what she was doing, she rolled her hips once, twice, her overstimulated clit hitting the hard ridge of his cock, and she shattered.

A scream tore from her throat as wave after wave of pleasure crashed through her.

Taron kissed her, swallowing her cries, and his touch grew rough on her skin. He prolonged her orgasm, pinched her nipples, and rocked his hips against her exactly where she wanted him.

When she quieted, he held her close.

"You tricked me," he grumbled. "I wanted to make it last."

Adriana stretched beside him like a cat. "Mm. It was so

worth it." She peered up into his eyes. "This was amazing. But..." She rose above him and nudged him. "Flip to your stomach. I want to try something."

Taron quirked an eyebrow and pointed at the front of his pants. The impressive bulge there almost made her reconsider her plan. But she was too curious to let him distract her.

"If I'm right, you'll thank me," she added with a grin. "Now, flip."

He muttered darkly but obeyed, and Adriana moved to straddle his hips, his taut ass beneath her. In front of her was his broad back, the spikes of his spine and shoulders startling in their strangeness.

She touched the low bump just above his waistband. Taron went very still below her. With the pad of her thumb, she rolled the small crest and caressed his cool skin.

She wasn't sure Taron was breathing, but he didn't stop her, so she continued on to the next spike, which was a quarter of an inch taller. To the touch, they weren't much different from human vertebrae; his skin moved over the bone.

Yet with every second, Taron's large body grew more taut, and his skin turned a deep, rich blue.

Finally, he groaned, as though he couldn't hold the sound back anymore. "Fuck. Adriana."

She grinned and massaged the dip between two spikes. "Do you like it?"

"I've never..." Taron fell silent, his breaths speeding up. "Ah, this feels so good."

Adriana stilled. "What do you mean, you've never?"

Taron turned his head to the side and looked at her from the corner of his eye. "When I touch my spine, it's just skin and bone. But your touch..."

She pursed her lips. "Do you think it's the warmth?"

He shuddered beneath her, his hands gripping the sheets as though he was barely holding himself back, but didn't answer.

Adriana's mind filled with wicked possibilities. "If I'm the only one who can do this for you..." She leaned down and brought her mouth to the tall spikes between his shoulder blades. They were almost as tall as her hand, and she wrapped her palm around one and stroked up, then ran her tongue over the tip.

Taron's hips moved beneath her: he was grinding them into the bed in rhythm with her pulls and licks.

Adriana reveled in the harnessed power of him—he was completely at her mercy, but only because he'd decided to trust her, to allow her to explore. She caressed him in earnest now, playing with pressure. Her core throbbed with need, with the desire to make him experience the same kind of bliss he'd wrought from her earlier.

Suddenly, Taron twisted below her, and she would have flown off him, off the bed, if he hadn't caught her in a crushing embrace. He sat up, bringing her to his lap, and crashed his lips on hers.

Adriana surrendered and opened her mouth to him.

With rough tugs, Taron ripped her underwear from her body, first the bra and then her panties. He lifted her up enough to free his cock, then lowered her, impaling her on his thick, cold length.

Adriana screamed in pleasure. Her senses were overwhelmed; Taron's hands were everywhere, driving her up and down so his cock plunged deeper and deeper, stoking the fire that never ceased to burn for him. He pinched her nipples until she thought she couldn't take it anymore, then soothed them with his cold, clever mouth.

"I want you to come all over me," he rasped into her ear. "I feel your hot little body melting for me."

Adriana sobbed, incoherent, "Yes, oh, Taron, yes!"

On instinct, she threw her arms around him, clinging on to him, a drowning woman clutching a life raft in the turbulent ocean of want. She closed her fingers on his spikes, and Taron's hoarse roar reverberated around the room.

"Adriana!" he shouted, his hips lurching up, again and again.

She came so hard, her vision blurred and the world around them ceased to exist. Her inner walls clamped down on his cock, the pleasure more intense than anything she'd ever imagined.

Taron's orgasm went on and on, a cold, addictive force inside her, and he toppled her to her back to fuck her through his aftershocks. She still clung to him, caressing him, gentling her touch, as she moaned in ecstasy.

Eventually, he stilled above her, his great chest heaving. Adriana put her palms to his cheeks and smoothed her thumbs over his high, sharp cheekbones.

"I love you," she whispered.

He rested his forehead on hers and closed his eyes. "I love you, too."

Adriana's heart swelled, and she opened her arms to him. He slipped out of her, but instead of lying in her arms, he pulled her to him and enclosed her in his cool embrace. She listened to the drumbeat of his slowing heart.

"Taron?" she muttered.

"Mm?" His voice was a rumble below her cheek.

She chewed her lip. "So this is your room..." She trailed off, not sure how to ask what was bothering her. She didn't have any possessions on Rendu apart from the luggage she'd brought with her from Earth. Would that bother him?

He chuckled. "*Our* room, Earthling. And don't freak out. We'll figure everything out. Now, rest, or that doctor of yours will know you disobeyed his direct orders."

Adriana grinned against his skin. "Yeah, I don't think he'll be fooled. Your caveman routine earlier didn't leave much room for interpretation."

Taron lifted his head a fraction to glare at her. "What's a caveman?"

Adriana opened her mouth, then closed it again. She thought for a moment. "You know what? I have so much to tell you. And you'll have to teach me all about—mmph."

Taron silenced her with two gentle fingers over her mouth. "Tomorrow, you can tell me about the cavemen and the Chris-must, and I'll show you around the house. But right now, you need to rest. I'll want another round of this soon." He swatted her naked backside.

Adriana squeaked. "Okay, okay, I'm done." With some wriggling, she buried herself under the smooth sheets. "But you better get some sleep as well. I have plans for you."

Taron hummed and drew her close, her back to his front. He tweaked her nipple, and his hardness pressed between her legs. "On second thought, we can sleep later."

Laughing, Adriana turned her head toward him, claiming his lips in a slow, sensual kiss. They had all night to explore each other's bodies—and more, they'd have their entire lives to spend together. She closed her eyes and let Taron take her apart, one rough, loving touch at a time.

EPILOGUE

Taron

FOUR YEARS later

"I swear, if you try to carry me over to the sky port, I'll punch you in the throat, Taron."

Adriana was waddling along the cleared road. She'd refused his offer of taking a hover sled because she wanted to get some exercise.

Now Taron was doing his best to restrain himself, but all he wanted was to grab her and protect her from falling.

"I know you said you didn't want that hover sled, but..." he began.

"No!" She stopped, her hands at her hips. Her round belly strained against the laces of her coat. "I'm pregnant, not sick. Now come on, they'll be here soon."

Taron sighed and followed her. He looked down at his front, where their firstborn, a year-old daughter with black hair and pale, blue-tinged skin was strapped in a carrier on his chest. She was born on the night of a wild ice storm, and they'd named her Lila. She was the most perfect mix of Adriana and him, somehow resistant to cold despite her warm, soft skin.

"Your mama knows best," he murmured and kissed her head, then held out his hand to help Adriana over a patch of ice.

She grumbled but took it, and together, they made their way toward the low hangars.

Taron was happy, happier than he ever remembered being in his life. His family was growing, and he thought he might like two or three more babies before long. He wasn't certain Adriana would agree—and had to admit he didn't know human women got so *round* when carrying their young. She was splendid in her pregnancy, and he worshipped her body every night to show her how much he loved her.

"Why did they have to come *now*?" Adriana muttered as she ascended the steps to the hangar's door. "They couldn't have waited another three months, oh, no. Now my mother will want to do checkups and poke me and...*ugh*."

Taron wisely didn't say anything. They'd been over this conversation several times since Adriana's parents announced their imminent arrival with the next ship flying from Earth to Rendu. The trade route was established, though not many humans were permitted entry to the planet. Even Adriana's parents wouldn't be staying—not that they'd expressed any wish to do so.

Taron hoped they would finally realize what they lost when Adriana decided to stay here. Adriana didn't think their indifference was strange, but Taron knew otherwise. If they so much as hinted that she or their children were anything less than flawless, he would pack them off on the very next spacecraft to leave Rendu, even if it was a rica transport ship.

"Quick, how do I look?" Adriana asked.

She took off her knit hat, so Taron smoothed some flyaway hairs from her face. "You're perfect," he replied. Then he kissed her, mindful not to squish Lila or the baby bump between them, but poured all his passion for her into every stroke of his tongue, every caress of his lips. Adriana held on to him, giving him back everything. That was just how she was, his human.

Someone cleared his throat nearby.

Adriana jumped back, her cheeks flushing red. "Oh!"

She turned and faced the two newcomers. The man and woman both had black eyes and the same dark hair, though her father's was cut short and her mother's was tied back in a severe bun. Adriana's hands flew to her mouth, and for a moment, Taron thought she was going to freak out.

Then she glanced back at him and extended her hand. Stepping forward, Taron took it, and gave her fingers a light squeeze.

Adriana sucked in a deep breath, smiled, and said, "Mom, Dad, I'm pleased to present to you Taron ad Naals, Captain of the Royal Fleet, Chief of Foreign Affairs...and my husband."

It was that last role he cherished most dearly.

Thank you so much for reading *Cold Attraction*! I hope you enjoyed Taron and Adriana's story.

I wrote a special Valentine's Day freebie just for you - it's

Taron and Adriana's first time celebrating, and Taron is understandably confused! What is a Valentine, and why is Adriana making a fuss about it? Get the free short story right here (or write me an email and I'll send you the link!).

You can also grab **Cold Temptation**, Mika and Kol's story on Amazon!

I'd be super grateful if you wrote a quick review of the book on Amazon, Goodreads, or Bookbub! Reviews help authors so much.

Thank you!
Zoe

ACKNOWLEDGMENTS

I know not everyone reads this part but I love writing Acknowledgments. It's a place to remember all the great people who helped (in big and small ways) to create this book.

Thanks to my critique partners, Jolie and Elle, for their support, funny comments, and daily chats (and to Elle for the amazing cover). Let's see how these aliens do in the real world!

Thanks to Betti, who inspires me to write more and is the best role model. The next coffee is on me!

I'm grateful to the wonderful team of people who beta read, edited, and proofread this alien story without batting an eye: you're the best. This book wouldn't be here without you.

I'm also forever thankful for my two boys who love space-ships but still have trouble understanding that the Sun is, in fact, a star, and that we're just a tiny speck in the vast Universe. I hope you know that I love you to the stars and back.

And a big thank you to my husband, who loves SciFi so much, he passed the affliction to me. Without you, I might never have thought of ice planets and dangerous enemies. Thanks for being my sounding board and my rock.

ABOUT THE AUTHOR

Zoe Ashwood is a romance writer with a passion for suspenseful stories with a sexy twist.

While she's always been a reader, Zoe's writing used to be limited to diary scribbles and bad (really *bad*) teenage poetry. Then she participated in NaNoWriMo 2015 and never looked back.

When she's not writing, Zoe works as a literary translator. She's happily married to her best friend and has two small boys who are as stubborn as they're cute.

She's always super happy to hear from fellow bookworms, so don't hesitate to get in touch! Her newsletter is an especially great way to stay up-to-date with all the latest news (and get a free book).

ALSO BY ZOE ASHWOOD

Trust the Wolf - shapeshifter paranormal romance
(a three-book series)

Give Me a Day - clean contemporary romance
(a three-book series)